HUNTED BY THE WINTER KING

A FAETED MATES NOVEL

ARIEL HUNTER

Hunted by the Winter King
Ariel Hunter
Published by Ariel Hunter
Copyright © 2019, Ariel Hunter
Edited by ALD Editing
Cover Art by Mibl
All rights reserved under the International and Pan-American Copyright Conventions. No part of this book may be reproduced or transmitted in any form or by any means, electronic or mechanical, including photocopying, recording, or by any information storage and retrieval system, without permission in writing from the publisher.

This is a work of fiction. Names, places, characters and incidents are either the product of the author's imagination or are used fictitiously, and any resemblance to any actual persons, living or dead, organizations, events or locales is entirely coincidental.

Warning: the unauthorized reproduction or distribution of this copyrighted work is illegal. Criminal copyright infringement, including infringement without monetary gain, is investigated by the FBI and is punishable by up to 5 years in prison and a fine of $250,000.

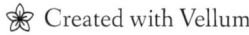 Created with Vellum

NOTE TO THE READERS

Thank you for taking a chance on me and reading my debut book. The world of Faerie is one I've fallen heads over heels in love with and I can't wait to show you how deep the magic, the bonds, and secrets all run. Thank you.

MARA

A ragged, worn cloth circled the counter for the fifth time that evening. Mara turned to humming along to the music as she cleaned. The Beatles had never failed her on a night where the rest of the world neglected to show up. She looked down, letting out a small sigh when she realized she was taking off the wood's varnish.

The record continued to spin, old and well-loved. Perhaps 'previously enjoyed' was a better description for anything in the overcrowded-but-spotless antique shop. Mara tossed the rag aside with the cleaning supplies and rested on the counter by the till. She pulled a container of Twizzlers towards her, stealing a few to chew on as time crawled. With nothing to entertain her on a drizzling, miserable night like this, she felt like just another piece in the shop.

Mara didn't like cleaning by any means, and

normally the store wouldn't be this spotless. But not a soul had walked through the doors all day and she'd closed hours ago. Sometimes, in a bustling city filled with lights and gawdy attractions, people failed to realize the real treasures right before their very eyes. Every piece was important to Mara. Every piece had a story.

The shop was filled to the brim with knickknacks. A brass compass, piles of old books, and handfuls of tiny trinkets were displayed for sale. Wooden chairs, bundles of herbs, and cast iron bells all had their place. Everything but the hand-carved cuckoo clock that chimed every hour. Yeah, that one could go. That stupid clock was just a painful reminder of time passing with no income. The last call from the bird was half an hour ago, twelve lonely chirps in a row. Mara couldn't even justify what she was still doing up.

She opened the till once more, drawer sliding open with a mechanical whirl. Anything change? Nope, nothing. Could the calendar lift her spirits? She turned from the counter, resting her elbows back behind her. Big red Xs crossed off the passing days and a golden retriever puppy sat opened mouthed in a field of hay. Her hazel eyes scanned the days, noting the date circled next week.

"Shit," she cursed under her breath. It sucked when working hard gave you nothing to show but the weight of living and rising bills. If she could just clear her inventory of some of her bigger items, then maybe she had a chance of meeting the rent. Hopefully.

The door chimed behind Mara and she didn't bother to move. She'd closed up anyways and had convinced herself that she was hearing a customer when they weren't there. When the shuffling of feet confirmed someone had entered, Mara inwardly groaned. She had forgotten to lock the door. Who came into a shop past the midnight hour?

Mara quickly pushed aside the fact that she had been standing at the counter most of the day, waiting desperately for a customer to show up. But anyone coming in this late was either drunk or a creep that wanted her number. She couldn't be so lucky for a patron with cash that wanted to lowball a price for an expensive artifact . . . or perhaps someone looking to shop from the back.

"Sorry, we're closed. Didn't flip the sign," she called from over her shoulder. Mara took a copper statuette in her hands, dragging an old stool over with the tip of her foot. "We open tomorrow at ten." She stood up on the step, carefully placing the item on the back of the top shelf. She was tall enough to reach it on her own, but it was a strain and not worth putting the little figurine in danger.

"That's a damn shame. Thought you would be interested in this one." The man's voice was playful as he stepped into the light, his smile mischievous in nature. His tall, wiry stature was cloaked by a black trench coat that went down past his knees. He wore a matching deerstalker that tucked away his own fiery red curls, his beard kissed by droplets of rain.

Mara almost lost her footing at the recognition of the voice, quirking a brow as she jumped down to face him. Her lips pressed together in a thin line. "Well, well. If it isn't lousy Lou." Her hands settled on the curve of her waist, tilting her hips to the side.

"Aye, I deserved that. Mara the mighty pain-in-my-ass. See, we can all do nicknames, ya' fiery ginger."

"Takes one to know one. And that hat looks ridiculous on you. You look like Sherlock Holmes."

"You don't like it? I wore it just for you, lass."

The woman fought the emotion playing on her lips, biting down on the side of her tongue. As much as she admired her friendship with Lou, he had done her wrong. "You're not welcome here, Lou." She swallowed, holding her ground as she narrowed her eyes on the leprechaun. "That last gig of yours screwed me over big time. Two months of rent, man. If I don't—"

"If you don't what? Get the cash?" he said, taking another step towards the counter. He held his hands up in a truce, as if it was all he needed to do to be forgiven for past indiscretions. "Relax. I wouldn't show my face to you if this wasn't good money."

Mara had half a mind to kick him out the door. The Beatles record was no longer playing, a lazy static circling the air. She contemplated his words before carefully asking, "How good?"

"More than double the last." Lou took a step to the side, picking up a pair of antique bone dice. He rolled the hand-carved trinkets as Mara contemplated his words. Double would fix her rent problem . . . but was it worth it? The dice clattered against the counter, coming up with snake eyes. Lou looked up at her slyly. "Far more than double."

Mara bit her bottom lip, moving the dice to the side so she could think without him distracting her. Lou frowned, but awaited her decision. "Give me a number."

"A hundred grand. Cash." Lou leaned his hip on the side of the checkout, watching in amusement as she let out a soft whistle. Mara knew that Lou wouldn't joke about this. Leprechauns were serious about money. Especially Lou.

Even if she got screwed over again, even if it were half as much . . . she would be able to catch up and then some. Mara silently turned, eyeing up the calendar. Her gaze flitted to the circled date and then to the puppy. She licked across the bottom of her tiny-fanged teeth.

"It could maybe, I don't know . . . cover those two measly months of rent with a wee pocket change to spare?" Lou pushed, teasing the idea once more.

"A little? Yeah, just a bit. You sure this gig is real?"

Lou straightened up at the accusation, placing a hand over his heart. "I swear on me mum's grave. It's as real as I am." For a mythical creature in a mundane world, that answer wasn't as reassuring as Mara hoped it would be.

To be honest, maybe it was just how lightheaded she felt by the amount. That number was . . . unthinkable. Cover up those two months of rent and be four more ahead? Get a dog that she could take care of? A final glance at the puppy on the calendar and her heart was sold. After a long moment of silence, she finally spoke up.

"What do I need to find?"

There was a glint in Lou's eyes as he chuckled, unbuttoning the top few closures of his coat. "For that price, it's not what you need to find, but *who*."

Mara paused for another moment, her dreams of stability and puppies put on hold to the harsh reality. This was a bounty on a person. Not an artifact. It wasn't surprising by any means, and she'd done it before . . . but still. The price tag came with danger. Lou reached in, grabbing a sealed wax envelope and holding it out towards her. Once Mara took the parcel, the hunt would begin.

The woman breathed in deeply, reaching across the counter and taking it from his hands. She pushed away the feeling of dread as it clawed and crawled up from the bottom of her stomach. As her thumb slipped under the wax seal, the door to the shop chimed. Lou was already on his way out. He paused by the door, flipping the sign of the shop to "closed."

VARECK

The Winter King of Faerie stood against the railing of the castle's snow-covered balcony. His broad shoulders rigid beneath a cloak of fur; body unmoved by the cold. Piercing blue eyes were scrutinizing the frozen tundra before him. Looming, malicious clouds lingered behind snow-capped mountains.

"This land is barren and desolate." The words fell from his lips with mild venom, gloved hands clenching the rail. King Vareck allowed his eyes to close, breathing out slowly, the warmth of his breath dying as the frigid air turned it, the small puffs curling around his sharp cheekbones in wisps.

Through his daily life, he could feel the frozen landscape chipping away at his heart. But, more importantly, he was losing the sensation in his toes. He impatiently turned to the door as he heard the creaking of old wood from behind him. A group of four hurriedly entered towards the king, footsteps crunching in the newly fallen snow.

"You made me wait, Lorne." His stiff words were betrayed by the slightest smile. It disappeared as soon as it had appeared. The king's long, brown hair draped over his shoulder as he turned to view the intruders of his morning respite. A light snow had begun to fall, clinging to his eyelashes and the fur of his cloak. Three of the four were guards of the king, dressed in black leather armor with smaller pieces of ornate ebony steel. The lightest bit of golden trim aligned their uniform and the seal of the king sat faithfully on their shoulders. Each one was adorned with a sword or bow by their side.

Next to the guards stood an older dark fae. His silvery gray hair was shorter at chin-length, slicked back without a single strand out of place. He wore heavy maroon and black robes with a matching scarf, and a bundle of leather books piled under his arm. A dimple on the left side of his face exposed itself as he offered his own small smile to the king.

"Apologies, Your Grace." Both he and the guards bowed. Each of their left hands moved to their chest in fists, in salute of their kingdom. As Lorne stood properly, he continued his words. "The ice takes longer to melt off my old bones these days." The steward stretched his neck out to the side, bringing out the book from beneath his arm. Reaching into his robes, he pulled out a quill.

Lorne scribbled once, twice, licking the nib of the quill to get the ink to flow. He tilted the book to stop the flakes of ice from getting onto the paper. "How may I assist you, my king?"

The King remained in the open snowfall, letting the cold seep in. "I need you to make arrangements for a social gathering. It will be held within the castle ballroom. Mark the date in a week, after the next full moon." He paused, turning his gaze towards the wasteland once more. "The event will be a masquerade. Yes, something grand enough to bring them all in attendance and I won't need to see their faces."

The steward almost dropped his pen, adjusting his thin-framed glasses at the Vareck's frank phrase. "Forgive me, is there a celebration of sorts that I'm misremembering?"

"More of an announcement."

"An announcement?" The steward hesitated more with each statement, glancing between the king and the guards.

Vareck paused to consider his words. His tongue moved to wet the top of his bottom lip. "Yes. I will be abdicating to the royal court." There. He said it. Let it be known. The guards on the balcony stilled as Lorne closed his book. The sound of silence was almost deafening.

"B-but, Your Majesty—"

He turned back to face the group directly, his words stern, his dark brows clenched inward. "This is not an open debate, Lorne. I respect everything you have done for my family, but this is my choice."

"I . . . I cannot—will not—accept this. Your, your nephew . . . he is not fit to—"

"I will only repeat myself this once. At the masquerade I will be renouncing my claim to the throne. It is what the people want." Vareck's voice grew strained, but his demeanor remained as cold as the chill.

"B-but, Your Majesty!" the steward gasped.

"You are dismissed." It was the end of the conversation. The steward shook his head, shoulders drooping as he gazed up. Vareck raised his hand, waving him off. The guards shifted, an uncomfortable moment of hesitation before faithfully leading the steward away. Only one knight remained behind.

Her blonde hair was neatly pulled back into a high ponytail. The clean look exposed her frost-kissed pointed ears, high cheekbones, and brilliant blue eyes. The door to the balcony closed and all that remained were the king and his most faithful knight. They stared eye to eye until she was the first to break. "May I stay to chat, Vareck?"

His lips curled into the slightest smile, this one lingering for a little longer. He let out a defeated sigh, patting the spot of the railing next to him. "Only for being smart enough to drop the title. You may stay, Kaia." A silence stood between them as the snowflakes fell and the knight slowly made her to stand next to the king. They both looked out at the open valley as a gust of wind played with the ends of the Vareck's hair. He didn't know how long she was going to stand there and let him stew.

"Alright. Get it over with, Kaia."

"Get what over with?" Her tone was innocent; gentler than you would expect for someone in full armor. "When I look out at the open land, something tells me that we might not have the same view."

It was an entertaining concept to think about. Certainly, she was looking at the same hellscape as he. "Physically or figuratively?"

"Perhaps both," Kaia answered cryptically. "Tell me what you think of it."

He scoffed. "What I 'think' of it . . ." He let out a long sigh, letting go of his proper stance. He let the bracers on his arms feel the cold bite as he leaned forward on the stone railing. "You are my dearest and oldest friend, Kaia. You always will be, before and after the crown."

"After is what currently has my full concern," Kaia said, lips pressing into a thin line. "I understand that you feel the need to move on. And please, don't misunderstand. I will follow you until the very end, Vareck. Crown or not," she added, her words complimenting his previous. "I am the sword at your side. But to serve you best, I need to know. Is this . . . what you really want?" She turned to face him.

"Yes. It is. I cannot restore the empire my father

has destroyed, try as I might. I'm so tired, Kaia. The fertility issues, dying crops, never-ending winter. The greenhouses suffer and can't meet the needs of the population. The people starve and use my name as a curse. I no longer blame them for hating me." He lets out a small huff of a laugh, defeated in nature. "That used to fuel me, Kaia. I pushed myself, did everything I could . . . and for naught."

"Vareck, you are not to blame for the weather. Every action you have ever taken has been for the good of the people; your people. I beg you, please don't give up."

Vareck silently brooded over Kaia's words, taking a long pause before shaking his head. "Perhaps not." He turned from the balcony, adjusting his cloak before rolling his words around his tongue.

He reached up, resting his left hand on her shoulder, squeezing lightly on a part of the leather. "Your console is welcome, but my mind has been made." The storm echoed loudly against the balcony walls as the intensity of it grew. Heavy flakes began to fall as the wind rose. Vareck regretfully let go, receding his arm back under his cloak.

There was nothing to say that could change his mind. There was no one in this world that could make him think or feel differently. Vareck accepted that his fate had been written as he headed back inside. Not even the largest fireplace in the castle could bring back his warmth.

MARA

"I swear, by the demons in every hell . . ." Mara spewed curses from under her breath, touching up her foundation with a powder brush in the mirror. Strands of ginger constantly fell out of place as she moved. She stopped every few moments to pin back her wild hair. Another curse slipped her lips, followed by a hiss as her hand moved across and smudged the lining underneath her eye.

The woman pointed a stern finger at the mirror of the bathroom lounge, wagging it with vigor in the direction of her reflection. "If you don't lock the door the next time Lou comes around, he's a dead leprechaun and it'll be all your fault." Of every living creature to ever exist, her target just had to be fae royalty.

"Why? Why did you take that envelope, Mara?" The question was rhetorical. She already knew the answer. Money. No wonder Lou ran off before she had the chance to read the fine print. The halfling fae figured she should have known better. A higher price was meant for a higher-profile target. She shook her head.

"I'm already here . . . no use backing out now." Her reflection nodded in agreement before taking in a deep breath. Mara glanced towards the door, an instant relief moving through her. The last thing tonight needed was someone to walk in on her embarrassing pep talk. Focusing back on her appearance, she adjusted the pleated, floor-length gown on her figure. Her hand pressed against her upper thigh, moving the slit in the skirt of the dress to cover a glint of silver.

A dagger hid itself away, strapped to Mara's leg. The bounty on Prince Sebastian involved getting him to the barrier alive. But it never hurt to be prepared in the most heavily guarded place on this plane of existence. She swallowed dryly.

Mara's hands moved up the silky onyx and ruby ombre dress, tightly fitted to her form. A black band sat snuggly at her waistline, hugging her curved hips. The front of the gown was graced with an open halter keyhole cut, connecting back up with the band at her neck. She turned her hips, tilting her head in the mirror. Just enough cleavage to be classy at a royal ball but still seduce her target. It was perfect, but it had cost her upfront what little money she had.

The huntress picked up her black clutch from the

counter, shifting through its contents. She moved a pair of magical handcuffs to the side, grabbing the much-needed eyeliner to fix her racoon eye. After everything was just right, it was time for the final piece: her mask. Red velvet with faux rubies slipped onto her head, tightened by a band in the back, black feathers protruding from the corner. With the price of the dress, she had settled for grabbing the mask from a cheap human costume store.

Just as everything was in place, the bathroom door opened. A woman entered dressed head to toe in pink frills. Even her mask seemed to match, the edges bunched as rose engravings adorned the material. Mara smiled politely, giving a small mutual nod that the space was open for use. She grabbed for her clutch, wrapping the band around her wrist as she pushed past the pink lady. "Excuse me."

At least the king's masquerade had given her the perfect opportunity. This would be her one and only chance to grab her target. An event like this was practically unheard of. Who knew when the next event in the castle would happen? Mara focused back on the task at hand as she headed into the main ballroom. The castle was flooded with guests, excited chatter and gossip circulating through the crowds.

"What do you think he'll be announcing?" One man opened the question to his group, wearing a simple mask carved out of oak.

"Do you think he's trying to marry?" a woman in a

yellow, poofy ballgown seemed to stutter with her growing excitement.

"Oh, it must be true!" another exclaimed. "He's definitely found a suitor. He's far too handsome for a cold bed." The merriment of the festivities seemed to leave everyone in good spirits, momentarily forgetting the troubles of the kingdom and the raging winter outside. Everyone but one.

Mara focused on not scrunching her nose at the gossip, eavesdropping for information about her target. None of the material was useful when groups only used time to talk about trivial things. Food was precious and only meager offerings were supplied, so guests around the her drank heavily while they laughed and danced along with the joyful live music played by the band.

A stranger stopped to grab Mara's hand, her breath catching in her throat. She watched, too stunned to move, as a shorter, plump man kissed the back of her wrist. He released, bowing deeply. "My dear, would you honor me in a —" She didn't hear him finish as she pulled her hand and vanished the moment he looked away.

Mara moved deeper into the crowd, grabbing a flute of wine from a tray held by a passing waiter. She didn't drink on the job, but this occasion certainly called for it. She tipped the glass back, taking a sip of the sweet liquid. It fizzled, tickling her throat in a familiar burning comfort. Nothing wrong with a little bit of liquid courage.

She was able to make it through the crowd a bit longer, inwardly cursing at the lack of appearance from the prince. She had been on the floor for at least half an hour, but all the masks made it nearly impossible to tell royalty from the average fae noble.

Another man in a black mask with a long beak took a few steps up to the ginger woman. Mara was now mentally prepared to react to the oncoming affections from the men in the ballroom. She pointed to the wine, downing the glass before giving the noble an awkward thumbs up. "Great wine," she said, as he opened his mouth to speak to her. "I need another drink. Here, hold this." Mara handed him the glass and left the man left in a stupor as she walked away to find another waiter. Seemed like this task was a two-glass job after all.

Each of the royal staff were easy enough to find. They wore onyx masks with a white shirts and black pants. A black handkerchief sat in their front pockets, emblem of the kingdom of Faerie embroidered with snow white thread. Mara stopped a woman with a tray, grabbing another small flute of wine. Sipping from the glass once more, she paused. A strange feeling crawled up her spine, tickling the hair on the back of her neck. She placed a hand there to quell the sensation, freezing the rest of her motions. While Mara stood still, the world continued to move, dance, and laugh. But there were eyes on her. The huntress was familiar with being the hunted.

Mara forced herself to move, gripping onto the glass in her hand. Her gaze circled the room slowly, searching for the source of her unease. The ballroom itself was simple, but luxurious. A large flat area was reserved for dancing, pillars lining the outer edge as it supported a second floor towards the front of the room. The back was lined with stained glass windows, a mural depicting the story of Faerie and its past kings. Every time a new king came to rule, part of the wall was carved out for a new portion of the mural.

In front of the glass, however, was a makeshift throne. And right there, sitting front and center, was the source of her troubles. King Vareck sat towards the front of the chair, hands gripping the sides of the armrests. His mouth opened slightly as he stared Mara down. She locked into his gaze, feeling the chill return deep in her chest.

She'd heard of the king before, and while it was his party and his castle, she hadn't expected his attention. His eyes were a beautiful but eerie piercing blue, long brown hair untamed beneath the crown. His broad shoulders seemed to tighten as Mara took a step back, quickly turning her gaze. Was the wine causing paranoia or did he pierce into her soul?

Did he know why she was here? Did he know what she was here to do? No. Foolishly impossible. Mara glanced down at the wine before setting it on part of the exposed architecture against the wall. One glass job. One glass job. She repeated the words in her head like a mantra as she tried to calm her nerves. It was impossible to get over the intensity of the king's gaze. Did he think she was someone else?

Another man in a wolf-like mask walked past, a girl with brunette hair on his arm. His strong jawline seemed to extend from the grin across his face. He leaned over, whispering a secret into the girl's ear as Mara did a double take. Wolf mask, dark hair, strong jawline . . . she observed what he was wearing, checking off every mental note on her list. With how lavish his outfit was and the smaller crown upon his head there was no question. The Wicked Prince had passed right in front of her and was headed out the large set of double doors.

Mara made the mistake of taking one last glance at the king, needing to confirm that it was a fluke. Only his gaze remained, even going so far as to push himself slowly off the throne and onto his feet. She quickly ducked into the crowd, mumbling to herself, "The prince. He was looking at the prince."

She needed to get lost in the sea of people, wrapping her arms around herself. Never in her short twenty-five years had she felt so out of place. Would she have wished that the king had given her that sort of attention? Mara slashed the idea from her mind, refocusing her thoughts. It didn't matter. She was a half fae orphan who owned a mostly human antique shop. Her name was Mara Wylde, and she had a bounty to collect.

Weaving through the sea of guests, she continued to rationalize until she felt secure enough of her displacement. There were only a few redcaps in the room, but hopefully that would be a sufficient distraction if someone was looking for her. The ginger shade of her hair was often mistaken for being a redcap, even if it was much lighter. Mara pushed away her childish, paranoid thoughts as she snuck into the hallway. Looking to the left, and then the right, the corridor was clear. All the guards had to be watching over the party.

Mara turned blindly down one hallway, then another, making sure she was out of sight from any wandering guests. Once she gotten far enough away, she breathed out slowly. "Where did you run off to, prince?" Focusing in on her power, the slits of Mara's eyes narrowed, the hazel color shifting and glowing a bright, vibrant green.

Her vision faded to black from the edges and she felt her spirit tug at her core, homing in on everything she knew about the prince. Images flashed in her mind as she put her whole concentration into finding him. Sebastian's voice was a low, deep rumble as he whispered to the woman about meeting him in another room. His smile was charming, quirked to the side. His hair was as dark as a forest in midnight, eyes almost as brilliantly blue as the king's . . .

Mara flinched, almost losing the trail. She

composed herself for a moment, taking a few more seconds until, "There you are." A smirked curved at the corner of her lips. She felt her path connect to Sebastian's spirit like a tether. No matter where he went, she could find him. Mara's head snapped towards the direction of the prince, eager for the thrill of the hunt.

She moved carefully through the palace's long hallways, almost not able to see the lights that danced and flickered from the glass chandeliers above. Everything was blurred and dark besides her direct path, causing Mara to tread lightly. All magic had its limitations that Mara had long ago realized she needed to respect. And yet, she couldn't help but want to rush through the castle. Something deep within her told her she was running out of time.

A hazardous set of stairs, avoiding three groups of guards, and almost knocking into a statue later, Mara spotted the prince up ahead. She sighed in relief, letting go of the tether as she approached. Finally, her eyesight returned to its normal state, the huntress blinking in relief. She smoothed out her dress as she stepped off the carpet. Her heels clacked on the marble, indirectly letting the prince know she was approaching.

"Prince Sebastian?" she called out, voice light and wispy. The prince paused, turning towards her. He looked curiously at her unfamiliar red mask.

"Well, hello. What a lovely little bird." The prince

gave her his most charming smile accompanied by a bow. "My deepest apologies. I must admit, I'm on my way to . . . meet . . ." his voice slowed, mouth held open slightly. Mara had moved in towards the prince, tugging down on the shoulder strap of her dress. She batted her long eyelashes beneath the mask, irises glowing once again that familiar bright green.

"You would like to meet me instead," Mara persuaded; voice feathery but firm.

"I think . . . I would like to meet you instead," the prince said. He shook his head, unable to turn away from her. She saw that he was entranced, finding it hard to swallow and pulling at the collar of his shirt.

Got you.

"How come nobody told me the kingdom of Faerie had such a handsome prince?" Mara purred, hand moving to hover near the dagger as she stepped forward. The prince followed the dance, stepping back until he found himself against the wall. He huffed out a laugh, wrapping both of his hands around her waist.

"Did no one? It's such a hard thing to miss."

"Very hard," Mara agreed, nodding her head before moving in for a kiss. The prince worked without pause, gripping his fingertips into her waist and bringing her closer to return the gesture.

VARECK

THE THRONE HELD AN ICY CHILL. Vareck sat at the front of the ballroom as the festivities took their course. His legs were spread out to the corners of the chair, leaning back to rest his check in the palm of his hand. He tried not to seem too bored as nobles approached and music floated through the background. But in a ballroom filled with so many people from Faerie, he had never felt so disconnected.

"Nobility at its finest." The words were cast from beneath his breath as the music paused. Men, women, and creatures of all kinds broke off from their dances and began to chat away. The band shuffled around at the front, the violinist taking a break to fix one of her broken strings. It was almost eloquent how swiftly the floor went from dancing to drinking and gossiping.

"King Vareck, you're looking exceptionally handsome tonight." A water nymph approached, gills and glitter lining the side of her neck.

"I say, this is the best party I've attended in ages. Wouldn't you agree?" another noble cooed.

"Yes, it's almost good enough to forget the chaos outside. Don't you think?"

The comments and questions were directed at Vareck, but with no response from him, they continued to drone on to one another.

Vareck nodded politely on occasion, but otherwise found it was best to ignore them. They were all just empty souls with blank faces. Strange masks that wanted something from him that he could no longer deliver. A hand found its way to his shoulder, Vareck glancing up to see Kaia standing faithfully at his side. She was dressed in formal guard's attire, the pieces of armor more decorative than functional.

"Mind your posture," Kaia leaned in to whisper, her voice playfully scolding. The king rolled his eyes, swatting away her hand. He knew her well enough to know she considered it a minor success.

Vareck's gaze returned out to the open ballroom, sighing as his eyes idly searched the crowd. He frowned to see the Sebastian out among them. Of course, his nephew was here to be the life of Vareck's own party.

Sebastian tilted his wolf mask up to wink at the two fae he was chatting up. He must have said something amusing because they were soon laughing. The blushing one almost spilled her wine. Vareck figured she must have had too much to drink to find Sebastian humorous. The woman held out her hand to the prince, his nephew taking delight in kissing the back of it. Vareck forced himself to look away as Sebastian took the other woman on his arm.

"What a disgrace," he huffed, moving to press a finger into his temple.

"I beg your pardon, Your Majesty?" a fae standing near the foot of the throne asked.

He looked down at the noble unsure of what to say. The fae stared up at him as if he had been carrying out a complete conversation . . . which—to be truthful— was probably the case. He looked to Kaia for help. He could see the mild annoyance in her eyes. A look he knew. And one that only she could get away with.

"He is speaking of your incorrigible brother-in-law, sir. The one you were just telling us about."

"Yes, your wife's brother. He is obviously a fool of the people," Vareck attempted to recover, his mouth moving on its own. "Just because he knows how to charm them, they see him as perfect." Kaia stole a glance towards the King but remained silent, the noble's face turning to excitement.

"Why, yes. I do agree," the man exclaimed, pleased to get such an answer out of the mostly quiet and stoic king.

In Vareck's mind, the words were held exclusively for Prince Sebastian. His nephew's level of charisma was mildly annoying. The man knew how to get what he wanted without being pushed over, all while making someone else think it was their idea when it failed. The Wicked Prince held up to his title, and he could do no wrong by the people.

"Those are my exact thoughts, Your Grace. It's like you—like you plucked them from my mind. How invigorating!" the noble continued to falsely praise the king over nothing. Vareck was slightly thankful that his input was relevant. If only so he didn't have to reply a second time. It wasn't until a few minutes later that Kaia took sympathy.

The guard stepped forward, placing a hand over her chest. "The king must now prepare for his speech."

"Oh, my. Yes. Thank you, Your Grace." The man stumbled over his words with a bow before giddily scurrying off. Vareck's shoulders dipped in relief, staring straight ahead.

"Well, you certainly made him the happiest man of the evening," she mused, returning to her position at his side.

"At least someone is enjoying the party."

"Any chance I'll see you on the dance floor enjoying it too? I believe the music will be starting again shortly."

"If hell melts, perhaps," Vareck quipped. "I would say when it freezes over, but we're already there."

Kaia pressed her lips together, holding back a huff of a laugh. "As you wish, my king."

The music began in the ballroom once again, filling the air with a lively spirit. The stars painted on the ceiling glimmered with each note, their shine reflecting off the large center chandelier. It was beautiful, stunning—and Vareck couldn't seem to enjoy any second of it.

High fae paired up in the ballroom, the rest of the creatures standing aside. Each couple went palm to palm, their free hands tucking behind their back. They turned in circles, switching partners as they went. It was an old, customary dance of the high fae saved for formal gatherings. But to Vareck it was nothing special. Just a tradition to get through at every event in his youth. There had been no cause for such celebrations in many years.

That was when it hit him. A strong note of citrus caused his nostrils to twitch and his eyes began to search the crowd. The air was fresh, like a new day of spring. Soft rain could have poured down in the room, clearing the earth of decay and ruin. It was enticing. No, it was *intoxicating*.

Vareck's eyes widened, pupils turning into thin slits as his icy blue gazed desperately scanned the crowd. The first thing he found was her hair. The vibrant red color reminded him of the morning dawn, bringing the warmth of a long, forgotten sun.

Surrounded by a crowd of people, she picked up a flute of Faerie wine, tipping the liquid back. Her soft, supple lips caressed the glass. Strands of ginger hair kissed her cheeks, having long ago freed themselves from the intricate braid pinned on the back of her head.

Her curved figure matched with pointed ears lead him to believe that she was either a tall redcap or a halfling. His wandering mind went blank as his gaze swept over her dress, the fabric opening at her chest and teasing a show of her bare skin. Did she know? Was it exposed just for him?

He felt his mouth turn dry. Her scent was as strong as if he had the woman in his arms, face burrowed into the crook of her neck. A fire simmered in his stomach, a new hunger burning away the ice at his core. There was no mistaking it. She was the light that would pull him away from this eternal, endless night. Her hazel eyes locked his blue, Vareck's hands gripping the arms of the throne. He quickly sat forward, but she gazed away.

"Your Grace?" Kaia questioned.

"Her hair . . . the embers in my hearth . . ." Vareck exhaled just to breathe in deeply again. "Her eyes . . . they are like fresh foliage from underneath the snow."

"Pardon?"

"I've never found a warmth like this before. I've found her, Kaia." He willed the woman to look back at him, to notice him.

"Vareck, what in the netherworld are you talking about?" Kaia whispered harshly.

The woman in the crowd followed his silent

command, turning to face him once more ... before disappearing in the crowd. Vareck's jaw turned stiff, too stunned to answer. His breath turned shallow, quick to school back his expression as he pushed up off the throne to stand.

He couldn't begin to comprehend what had happened. He was the Winter King, ruler of the realm and of all Fae ... and she ... she *walked*? No. She was his mate, and no subject would turn to ignore him. She was his.

"King Vareck?"

"Wait here." His tone was stiff, cold once more as he moved down the steps to the open floor. He let out a scoff, eyes scanning the crowd for red hair. He pushed past the sea of fae, inwardly groaning as he followed the distracting scent. The people of the kingdom move around him, making way for the king as he grasped down on a woman's arm.

"O-oh my! King Vareck?" the redcap asked, turning towards him and pulling off her mask. Her brown eyes looked up to him in concern.

"My apologies," he growled, letting go when he realized his mistake. Damn. Where had she run off to? Was that his only chance? He was collecting a few stares as his gaze flitted from one end of the ballroom to another. He couldn't lose her. He couldn't lose her before he had the chance to—

Citrus. A whiff of her scent floated past him, pulling his gaze towards the front entrance. The woman in question walked out past the double doors. His senses were on high alert, taking a step forward when the music began to play again and he struggled to traverse the crowd.

"Make way, move!" He finally used his voice to make demands, people parting like the sea. He got to the doors, breaking through a dancing couple to reach the hallway.

"Hey! You can't just—King Vareck . . ." The woman was quick to quiet her complaints, Vareck not even stopping to notice or apologize as he continued forward. Without the room's musk of scents and bodies, the smell of the woman was clearer. The path was easy enough to follow, Vareck moving up staircases and past groups of guards as he headed towards the royal chambers.

He breathed a sigh of relief. She hadn't left the castle. The courtyard was in the opposite direction. His heart pounded in his chest. Had she known? Had she known she was his? Yes, it had to be. He would find her was awaiting him, disrobed and her dress discarded on the floor. Her pale, ivory skin resting on silk sheets with her body stretched across the mattress. She'd be on display, breasts covered only by one of her hands, with the faintest blush spread across her cheekbones, her eyes looking to him, waiting . . .

Vareck swallowed back the saliva that formed at the continuing thoughts, more eager than ever to find his mate and claim her as his own. Her scent was stronger now, lingering behind one of the guest bedroom doors. He hesitated, if only for a moment, with his hand hovering over the knob before opening the room to face his fantasy . . . his future . . . his mate.

Reality was far harsher. There, halfway towards the bed and half-dressed, was his damned nephew kissing his mate. The two looked up at the door, her fingers paused on a button of the Wicked Prince's shirt.

"Uncle?" Sebastian managed to ask, the first to speak. But Vareck couldn't respond. A red mist descended over his vision.

MARA

HE TASTED like wine and bad life choices. She was familiar with the flavor. Mara tilted her head to the side, biting down on Sebastian's lower lip. The prince groaned, moving a hand to her face as he pulled her against him. His five o'clock shadow brushed her chin, tickling her skin. They had ended up in one of the side rooms, Mara intent on spiriting away soon. It was just that, well . . . couldn't she enjoy the perks? He wasn't a terrible kisser.

She wrapped her arms over Prince Sebastian's shoulders, clutch in hand as she moved in for another distraction. Her fingers fiddled with the bag's opening, aiming to get the magical handcuffs inside. Sebastian let out a low chuckle, moving back to unclasp the collar of his shirt. Mara had to quickly let go of her prize, bringing her hands back to her sides.

"Impatient, are we?"

She hummed in agreement, moving to assist him with one of the buttons as she planted another kiss. All was going according to plan. Until the door to the room opened and caught them by surprise. The heavy oak slammed into the nightstand revealing none other than the Winter King himself. Had this wild, deranged man known all along that she was after the prince? If Lou set her up . . . oh, he was a dead leprechaun. Sebastian took a step away from Mara, wiping off red lipstick from the corner of his mouth.

"Uncle?" Sebastian managed to ask, the first to speak. "What's the meaning of this?" But the king didn't care to respond, storming in as he took the door and slammed it behind him.

"What are you doing?" the insane king snarled in her direction. Sebastian held up a hand towards him.

"Uncle, uncle. Calm down. This is . . . my friend."

"*Your?*" Vareck snapped, his hair tossing to the side as he turned from Mara to glare at his nephew. "She's your *nothing*." His auburn strands and sharp fangs almost reminded Mara of a lion putting a cub in his place. It would be alluring if she wasn't so close to danger. He pulled Sebastian to the side of the room, stepping between Mara and her target.

He stared at her, a feral look in his eyes. "I was talking to you." As best as she could tell, he managed to quell the flames of anger in his voice, if only by a little. He gritted his teeth, seeming to want to say more.

Letting out a frustrated sigh, he said, "Answer me. Now."

Persuasion. A gift that almost all high fae acquired. The same little parlor trick that Mara had used to seduce Sebastian was now being held against her.

She breathed out slowly, heart pounding in her chest. Mara took a step back, mouth trying to form the words as she fought them. He took a step closer as his eyes glowed blue. "Capturing my target." The words ungracefully spewed from her lips as she took step back, dodging around the side of a coffee table. Mara had been apprehended in a gig once before, but usually they didn't just . . .walk towards her with a . . . a look? Mara couldn't figure out the words to describe the king if she wanted to. With every step back he took a step forward.

"Wait, what?" Sebastian interjected. "Your target?"

"That's not what I meant. Why did you do it?" the Winter King asked, voice strained.

"Wait, what?" It was Mara's turn to echo the prince. The king tried to advance once more, Mara scrambling up onto the bed. She held one of the four posts, ready to skirt in the opposite direction of whatever the king chose.

"This is rather awkward. I think I'll just"— Sebastian took a step towards the door, pointing to the exit with his thumb—"maybe leave now."

"Sit." Mara and the king both turned to the prince, calling out the same word of command. They looked at each other, Mara mumbling, "jinx" underneath her breath. Numbly, the prince sat down on the edge of the bed between Mara and the king.

Vareck tried to get around the prince, groaning. "I want to talk to you."

"Sure, we can talk. From that distance." Mara hopped off the opposite side of the bed, cursing when her ankle rolled, a resounding crack popping from below. She prayed it was the floor and not her foot. This wasn't the sort of bedroom waltz Mara had in mind for tonight.

He took a step back, holding up his hands as he pleaded with her. "Just tell me. Why did you run when you saw me?"

Mara paused her game of cat and mouse, leaning against the bedframe. She tilted her head watching in wonder as he looked at her. His brows dipped, hand extending towards Mara.

The huntress took a slower step back this time, trying to comprehend his words. She was too confused to comprehend anything as he closed in. She took one step back then another, searching his face to try and piece together what he meant. Why had she run? She hadn't.

"You had nothing to do with it." Her breath caught in her chest and she accidentally backed into a dresser. The king didn't stop advancing. Even though her prey had been wearing a wolf's mask, the man before her was the wolf of the castle. She felt paralyzed as she stared at her with chilled, icy blue eyes.

Two sides of her were at war. The rational side scolded her; told her to use this opportunity to flee. Another side called to her animal instincts; those baser urges ingrained in our bones calling for us to give in to those impulses. She could feel her sister's words nagging in the back of her mind for being physically attracted to a man at an inappropriate moment and for that man being completely off his rail. Tall, dark, handsome, and a few screws loose? Shit, she guessed she did have a type, after all.

Mara found herself allowing the king to move in, unsure of what he was trying to achieve. Her hazel eyes scanned his broad shoulders, muscles hidden underneath the collar of his tunic. Her heart fluttered, breathing out slowly from her mouth as he palmed the dresses behind her on either side. His eyes hazed over as his nose pressed against her neck.

Nope. Nope. Nope. Alarms went off in Mara's head, fight or flight kicking in. The king moved in for a kiss, Mara swiping the blade from her thigh and slicing him across the side. What she expected would happen? He would move back, away, howl out in pain; something—anything. What happened instead? Nothing. Blood dripped off the blade's edge, Mara breathing out unsteadily as he silently inhaled. He didn't wince. He just stared at her with blown-out eyes. Another heavy breath left his lips, fangs extending. He moved in to kiss her once more.

"Stop, stop!" Mara cried out, eyes glowing their brightest, vibrant green. She didn't know if her magic could reach someone as powerful and apparently deranged as the fae king . . . but he stopped. Mara sheathed the blade, ducking out from underneath the king's arms and scrambled to stand next to Sebastian. Though under her persuasion, he still turned to numbly stare at her in wonder. Her magic had worked against him. Mara couldn't believe it. Neither could anyone else in the room.

"Stay. Don't move." She held out her hands, using her magic once more. "Good. Good boy, err- man . . . king? Good king." Mara was flying by the seat of her nonexistent pants, feeling a little light-headed at the continuous amounts of energy she used. Who knew how much it took out of her to tame the Winter king?

What the hell was going on? Mara felt the pressure of the situation crashing down on her. She was stealing the prince of Faerie and just stabbed the king. *Oh shit.* Her head snapped towards the prince, "Get up and follow me." She grabbed Sebastian by the back of his shoulder dragging him out of the room. She didn't dare look back. Mara figured she could process this entire clusterfuck after the money was securely wired to her human account. This all better be for the best damn dog in the world.

She pulled the cuffs out of her bag the moment she

had the prince in the hallway. Snapping them on his wrists in the front, Mara grabbed onto the center of the chain. A new way to pull him around. She moved to the left, knowing that she had to trace her steps back in hopes of getting out of this maze of a palace. Was it left, right, staircase, left? Or right, right, staircase, staircase?

"Are you lost?" the prince mused, gaining himself a glare.

"No, actually. Show me the way." Her eyes glowed, lip held to the side in a snarl. The quirky remarks were reserved for her. She didn't have time for a chatterbox prince.

"You could say please," he insisted, feet moving on their own as he took her back the way she came. Clearly it had been left, left, right, staircase, right.

"Now. Hurry," she insisted, pushing her limits once again. Mara felt the draining sensation of her power, not knowing how much longer she could keep up full command persuasion. There's a thick line between suggesting an idea and commanding an order. Mara was jumping back and forth across it.

"Yes, ma'am," the prince replied, completing her request in a hurry. Sebastian almost started to drag her along as he moved, a small pout sitting on the corner of his lips. "You seem like a really nice girl, you know."

"I'm not."

"Can we talk about this?"

"No."

"Do you really want to do this?"

"Yes."

"The king will have your head for this. He'll save me," Sebastian warned, moving to the left, down their second set of stairs. At the mention of the king, Mara felt her shoulders twitch, remembering the earlier proximity of his warm touch. She shook off the thought, returning to the task at hand.

The current corridor looked familiar. In fact, some of the guests could be seen up on the landing ahead, moseying their way out from the ball. Without the king nor the prince to keep the nobles entertained, they weren't sure what to do.

"Prince Sebastian?" a guard called out, stepping towards the two. Mara grabbed the prince by the cuffs, pulling him once again to the opposite direction.

"Run with me," she hissed commanding under her breath. The knight moved forward, calling out after them.

"Help! I'm being taken!" Sebastian called from over his shoulder.

"Shut up!" she hissed, cursing herself for not commanding him to do so sooner. Another guard from across the way heard, calling for the alarm.

"Don't let her escape! She's getting away with the prince!"

Mara yanked Sebastian by the cuffs. Turning sharply, she slid on her dress, heel snapping as it ripped across the bottom. She cursed, tearing away the bottom of her dress and kicking off her shoes.

"Get out of my way!" Mara called out, eyes flickering between bright green and hazel. She was losing her grasp on everything, wasn't she? The woman gritted her teeth, dashing down the hall with the prince in tow, dress bunched up in one hand. If anyone else said anything, she couldn't hear it. Her consciousness wavered, Mara stumbled once more out the main doors.

As the fresh air hit her senses, Mara inhaled deeply without stopping. She could hear the clanking of metal behind her. She made the mistake of glancing over her shoulder as she approached the courtyard. A blonde guard in the king's uniform called out orders to the rest of her squadron.

"Why are you doing this?" Sebastian struggled against the pull of her influence, the two approaching the fountain.

Mara looked at the prince, humoring him just this once. "Rent." The man wasn't as spoiled and pompous as she expected him to be. Still, she couldn't help but wish the king was in her cuffs instead of having to deal with this one.

Behind them the female guard called out once more, raising her bow. Mara didn't wait around to see how good her aim was, taking a deep breath before dragging Sebastian into the fountain. Where the prince had likely expected to meet water, she instead pulled him into another world.

VARECK

❋

"Stop, stop!" the woman cried out, Vareck coming back to his senses as a new overwhelming power washed over him. What was this feeling? He paused in his movements, the strange woman ducking underneath his arms. He had just enough will power to turn, trying not to lose sight of his mate.

He couldn't seem to comprehend her answer in his clouded, lust-filled mind. She ran because it had nothing to do with him? It had everything to do with him. He tried to reach for her, finding himself unable to advance. For his mate to possess so much power over him was . . . this woman was something else. Something he had never encountered before. Everything about her was thrilling; just being in her presence made him feel alive.

"Stay. Don't move." His mate held out her hands, using her magic once more. Her hazel eyes glowed and

Vareck couldn't help but stare into them numbly. "Good. Good boy, err- man . . . king? Good king." She tried to keep him at bay like some sort of animal. He gritted his teeth at the sight. Soon, she was grabbing his nephew by the collar, dragging him out of the room. She didn't even look back. Why did she even want Sebastian when he was there?

"I will find you, fae. There is nowhere you can hide from me." He wouldn't let the first encounter with his mate end like this. It was either a mistake or there was some sort of reasonable explanation for why she wasn't as attracted to him as he was her. She was his, and he would make it so.

He placed a hand over the wound on his side, barely feeling the burn as adrenaline pumped through his veins. Vareck held onto every footstep as the sound of the two faded down the hallway. He closed his eyes, focusing in on the noise. He had to move. He had to stop them. He had to bring her back.

The king winced, feeling the connect of his mate slip away. The smell of citrus, the warmth of the sun from the early morning dawn, it all faded to a familiar cold numbness at his core. His eyes shot up towards the door, forcing his foot forward, then another. His fangs extended past his bottom lips with a snarl.

This strange fae woman—his mate—was his last chance of redemption in this world. Fate had brought her to him tonight, and he could not afford to let her go. He cried out again, putting all his will into moving forward one foot, then the other, until he was out the door and down the hallway. A staggering snap cut into his chest, and the king stumbled. His hand clawed at his heart as the bond between him and his mate released. She was no longer in the realm.

"No!" He felt himself slipping away, only primal instincts remained as he tilted his head back to scream out. Vareck's eyes turned wild as he ran, trying to spot anything that could lead him back to her. The way her tongue moved in her mouth as she talked. The freckles that dusted her cheekbones. There were so many details he only had a moment to explore and each one drove him wild.

One glance from the king has guests in the front foyer scrambling to the side as he pushed through. Kaia stood up ahead, a scrap of fabric in her hand. Her eyes widened to see the king in such a state, deranged and bleeding.

"King Vareck, are you—" She didn't get the opportunity to finish her statement, the fabric forcefully taken from her hands. Kaia couldn't help but stare as Vareck burrowed his face into the scrap. He inhaled deeply, eyes rolling back.

"Where did you get this," he demanded; his mind satisfied for the moment as he grasped at every bit of their connection.

"The intruder, Your Grace," Kaia answered immediately. "We couldn't stop her. I couldn't stop her. I'm afraid she escaped with the prince through the fountain."

"The fountain?" Vareck inquired, the question almost in disbelief at the sight of the old relic in the courtyard. Even through the toughest of winters, it had been enchanted to not freeze over.

"Yes, our barriers of protection involve only the castle, not outside its walls," the guard confirmed. "You're injured. I'll call for a healer."

"No time. If she's that clever, the portal won't stick around." Vareck grunted as he ripped the fabric further. He tied the piece around his wrist, letting the rest fall to the ground as he headed down the courtyard steps.

"King Vareck!" Kaia called after him, quickly following him down to the fountain. "What are you planning to do?"

The king sniffed the air, staring down into the spinning waters. "Do not follow. I'll be back."

"Vareck, you can't—"

"I am the king," he snapped, words fierce and more alive than they had been in ages. Kaia went silent, taking a step back as Vareck turned to the swirling pool. Without thinking on it further, he jumped through.

MARA

❄

The world around her was dark. Mara reached out; the chain of the handcuffs tight in her grasp as the void consumed her. Everything felt like it was crushing down on her, making it impossible to breathe. A small light formed ahead. The huntress eyed up her salvation, moving desperately towards the glow. Tonight was not the night for getting stuck between realms.

Mara strained against the weight of the void, her fingertips getting ever so close. A sudden rush of wind howled past her. She and the prince appeared back in the human world, slamming into the walls of a closet. Buckets, cleaning chemicals, and mops crashed down upon them in a chaotic mess.

A groan escaped the woman's lips, cursing as she knocked her shoulder into another shelf. The light from earlier had disappeared, the room pitch dark around them. Mara let go of Sebastian, reaching up and swatting at the chain that hung from the ceiling. A pull of the tassel brought light to the shabby janitor's closet.

To say that Mara was exhausted was an understatement. She was glad for the opportunity to catch her breath. At least the guard hadn't let loose the arrow. Or, if she did, it hadn't hit her. The prince sat sprawled out on the ground, covered in bottles and debris. A bucket sat atop his head. He reached up to pull it off, glaring up at Mara.

Sebastian spit out a full mouthful of water from the fountain, clearly displeased. "I see I'm working with a real professional." Mara gave a sheepish grin and shrugged. They were both soaked and out of their element, but hey. He was the one in handcuffs. Who cared if her methods were a little unorthodox?

"Alright, pretty boy," she sighed, tapping into her persuasion once more as a mild vertigo coursed through her. "Follow me."

Sebastian stood, grimacing as he kicked aside a bottle of bleach with his foot. He dusted off his shoulder, looking over with a charming smile. "So, you think I'm pretty? Pretty enough to let go?"

"Silence." Mara huffed, issuing another command. This gig would be the death of her. The woman steadied herself on her feet, rubbing her shoulder from where she had impacted. That would certainly leave a bruise in the morning. Gathering her senses, Mara could vaguely make out the low, heavy base rumbling from outside the door. She grasped for the handle, pausing to turn behind her and nudge the prince forward. "Welcome to the Witching Hour."

The door opened; releasing a thick fog that rolled across the cheap linoleum flooring. Glitter covered every surface like the herpes of the magical world. Lights flashed from the center stage. A pair of twin pixies currently held the limelight, their long green hair curled in ribbons down to the small of their back. They curved around a set of poles, breasts bare and black thongs the only thing to cover their slim, delicate bodies. The only thing besides their thigh-high glimmering black boots, that is.

A goblin at one of the tables drooled over himself, slumping into his large glass of ale as Sebastian's eyes wandered the room. Tables of patrons turned to Mara and the prince as they tried to traverse the busy crowd. Mara made her way to the back bar as one of the pixies climbed the pole, only to slide down it dangerously, stopping only just before the bottom. The move earned the performer a couple of wolf-whistles and dollar bills as she gave a nymph at the table next to her a wink.

"Amelia," Mara called out, trying to catch the bartender's attention. The bar was filled to the brim as a single woman walked behind in. Her hands moved through the air as bottles swooshed out towards patrons, filling their glasses. They moved on their own, animated to life as they dribbled alcohol across the bar.

The bartender moved her hands above her head,

crossing her wrists as she turned on her heel. Fire sparked from her hands, sizzling out like a small, contained firework. The group at the bar cheered, a few of them drunk but clapping at her performance.

"Amelia!" Mara tried again, waving her hand to get the woman's attention. The witch glanced to the side to see the fae, eyes brightening at the recognition. She moved the train of her long lacey dress aside, strolling over to the side of the bar with a bounce in her step. Potions continued to bubble, overflowing onto the floor as the witch divided her attention.

"Mighty Mara! Figured I'd see you tonight. Loulou's in the back waiting for ya'."

Mara huffed, rolling her eyes at the newly acquired nickname. Lou must have worked his charm on her.

"Who's your cute friend?" Amelia purred, glancing him up and down. She paused when she saw the cuffs, smirking. "Guess it's all work and no play tonight? Total shame. I'm kind of into the whole handcuff thing." The witch bit her bottom lip, flicking her wrist to the side. A curtain materialized on the wall next to Mara, opening to reveal a back hallway.

"Thanks," Mara grunted, pulling the prince forward. Sebastian opened his mouth to reply, only to be stopped at the pull of Mara's magic. He huffed, forced to walk through as Mara guided him. Room after room was filled with elite guests, talking over wine behind veiled curtains. The thin fabric was enchanted to act as a sound barrier to keep everything out or in, depending on which side you were on.

A sharp pain jabbed through her heel, followed by a burning sensation. Mara flinched, looking underfoot to see she had stepped in the remnants of someone's expensive ice wine. The bottle was broken nearby and the leftover contents sticky as she was cursing the heels that she had discarded. Red smeared the piece of glass as she dug it out of her foot and tossed it in the trash. "Watch your step."

It took a few more rooms until Mara saw the familiar face of Lou. Her earlier rage returned with a vengeance. There was a stranger next to him, standing with their hands together as the leprechaun smoked from an old, wooden pipe. Lou blew smoke out from his nose, ghosting the vapor back into his mouth before finally exhaling the cloud. He offered out the pipe to Mara, a shit-eating grin covering his face.

"Mara the Mighty," he laughed, raising his arm up to flex. "I knew you could do it, lass. No problems, I presume?" Lou leaned his elbow on the table, wiggling the pipe in his free hand as it was offered up.

Mara declined, careful with her words at the sight of a black handgun sitting on the table. "You are the worst leprechaun I have ever met."

"Aye! I'm most likely the only one you've ever met, love. That makes me the best too."

"Royalty, Lou? Seriously? Next time don't enter my shop unless it's triple." Mara gritted the words through her teeth, exhaustion fighting with her temper. She pushed Sebastian forward and the prince stumbled to sit down at the table. "I've had one hell of a night because of you."

The man next to Lou shifted, but he held up his hand. Sebastian looked between the three, eyes wide with anxious anticipation. "Relax, would ya? Seems like you're still in one piece. I wouldn't give you something you couldn't handle." Lou removed an envelope from his pocket, smelling the money through the paper and winking at her.

"If you screwed me over again, I swear—"

"Oh, calm your pretty self. You have too sweet of a face to make threats like that. Take the charm off him and the promised money is yours. You can pay the rent for that shop and we'll be out of each other's hair."

Mara let out a long, slow breath as she closed her eyes. A touch of relief crossed her as she released all binds of magic from Sebastian. Even the prince inhaled sharply, grasping at the table as his look turned wild.

"This . . . this was seriously over rent money? You weren't kidding?" Sebastian hissed as the envelope slid across the table. Mara caught the parcel before it hit the floor, giving the prince a shrug.

"I said as much, didn't I?"

"I am the prince of Faerie. Save me from this mad man and I can get you whatever you—augh!" Sebastian hissed as Lou grabbed the pistol on the table, whipping him on the side of the head. The prince's figure slumped in the seat, breathing out shallowly.

Lou looked up at Mara, a simple smile across his face. "Pleasure doing business. I suggest you leave now, lass."

The huntress held the envelope in her hands up to her chest, eyes darting between Lou and the prince. She silently took a step back, watching as the prince gritted his teeth. His gaze turned a bright, dangerous blue, voice as wicked as his name. "I command you to relea—"

Before the prince even had the chance, Lou brought the pistol down once more, rolling his eyes. The prince slumped to a full state of unconsciousness as Mara quickly turned away. What's done is done. She had the money. She did her part. The prince's fate was out of her hands.

Mara moved through the back, careful to avoid the broken bottle for the second time as the reality of the situation seeped deep into her brain. "Oooooh shit." While she was the one doing the bounty hunting, there was no doubt a bounty on her head now. Lou had sent her to do his dirty work and even the one hundred thousand dollars in her hands wasn't enough to feel safe.

People weren't objects. It was easier when she was hunting artifacts. Cutting ties was simple when they didn't have lives of their own. Yes, objects had their own history and stories . . . and powers, but they couldn't be beaten and held captive. To what fate did she just leave the prince?

"Focus, Mara," she hissed beneath her breath, making her way back to the bar. She shuffled through the cash, placing on the table what she owed Amelia for the portal. Before the money even hit the bar, a drink was slid her way. Mara glanced up to see the witch leaning against the counter, long black, sharp nails stirring around a drink of her own. The shot was bright orange, red candy crystals decorating the rim.

"A ginger orange specialty shot for my favorite ginger," Amelia grinned, giving Mara a small salute before tipping back her own glass. She raised the glass, giving a gracious nod before downing the drink. Huh . . . it was a two-glass gig after all. Mara walked out towards the front, Amelia cupping her hands to call out, "Next time . . . no shoes, no service!" It was followed by a giggle, the witch returning to entertain her clients.

Even with finally hailing a cab, it felt like forever until Mara walked through the front door to her apartment. She dropped the keys on the counter, pushing herself not to crawl onto her futon and fall into a deep slumber. "Every part of me is sore, I want ice cream, and I'm going to die." The words were groaned out, rolling from her lips. She continued to move as fast as her tired body would take her, pushing herself towards her closet. Finding a backpack and a duffle bag, she threw them down on the floor of her tiny studio setting.

She realized she needed to let her sister know she would be leaving.

Mara opened her phone, scrolling through her contacts until she found her older sister. Sadie's chat conversation appeared on the screen.

Mara [11:38 pm]: I was seen 2night. Packing. Gotta get outta herw.

Typos aside, Mara was sure that Sadie Wylde would understand what was going on. Her adoptive sister was truly her other half. While Sadie wasn't always fond of Mara's line of business, she understood that things could get hairy. Sadie's family—her family—had always welcomed her as a fierce trouble-hunting redcap, even if she wasn't by blood.

Sadie [11:40 pm]: Are you alright? Is someone following you?

As much as Mara wanted to call Sadie, tell her everything that went down, she knew that she didn't have the time. There was so much running through her mind. What was with the tension between her and the king? It was like some sort of electricity that pulsed through her, drawing her to him like he was the calm before the storm. While she feared his gaze, it was impossible not to be entranced by the icy chill behind it. The way he breathed into her neck made her want to—

Mara shook her head, pushing away the thought. She put down a shirt she was packing away in the bag to reply to Sadie before the girl decided to show up at her front door. Mara didn't live that far from her sister and throwing Sadie into this mess was the last thing she needed. The halfling breathed out of her nose, trying to calm her nerves as she took the time to type out a full statement.

Mara [11:43pm]: Yes. The way he looked at me. Something was up. I don't know. I just need to get out of here. Go into hiding for a little bit. I'll call you when I get to the ... place, okay?

She knew Sadie would catch her drift. Yet, she couldn't help to feel somewhat foolish. What, was the magical fae community going to track her phone and read her messages? No, they didn't mess with the human technology they found to be beneath them. Fae were missing out. Cellphones were great.

Mara walked back into the kitchen, counting through the money Lou had left her.

. . .

Sadie [11:45pm]: Yeah. I'll meet you there. Be careful, okay? I love you. <3

A small smile flicked across Mara's lips, shaking her head. In a way, it pained her to know that she was most likely stressing Sadie out over nothing. There was no way that they could track her tonight, and if she kept moving everything would be okay. Mara let out a long sigh, quick to text back. Her thumbs swiped over her phone screen.

Mara [11:46pm]: Yeah, yeah. Luv u too. Give me thre

The message sent early, phone slipping from her grasp as ever part of her body tensed. A hand clasped over her mouth, strong arms pinning her against a body. The more she struggled to move the stronger his grasp, her exposed skin from the ripped dress pressed against the somehow still ice-cold fabric of the intruder. A deep sense of despair washed over her, not needing to look to know who it was.

Sadie [11:47pm]: Mara?

Sadie [11:47pm]: Give you what?

Mara's phone buzzed against the floor with each unread message, a deep voice whispering in her ear as he let out a ragged breath.

"You don't get to run from me."

VARECK

Thick fog rolled through the air of the Witching Hour, his large figure cutting through the mist. The king snarled from the abrasive form of teleportation, dripping in fountain water and envy. Vareck moved through the strange crowd, not distracted by the quirky creatures that enjoyed their merriment. Was the limited visibility and smells of cheap booze and sweat truly the world of his mate? Or had he perhaps found himself in strange layer of hell?

The King took a moment to survey his surroundings, trying to gather a foothold on the situation. Who was the leader of this establishment? Who ruled amongst the drunken goblins and dancing naked pixies? Vareck approached the back bar, watching a woman play around precariously with fire. Soft notes of summer tingled his nose. He corrected his posture as he approached. It was doubtful that any of his intimidation tactics would work with the squelching of his wet boots across the cheap flooring.

Moving a hand through his hair, the king wrung out the excess liquid as he caught the bartender's attention. "Tell me, wench, have you seen a fae with fiery hair?"

The bartender turned and looked him up and down. "Wench?" she asked with a quirked brow, hand falling to rest on her hip. "You're definitely new around here. But if you leave a good tip, you can call me whatever you want. What can I get you? Tall, dark, and—" Her lips soured, homing in on the circlet upon his head, a look of recognition appearing on her face.

"You know what?" the witch said, tilting her head. "I haven't, but let me check if anyone in the back has seen your ginger fae." She held up her hands, slipping towards the back room.

Vareck didn't enjoy being told to wait. Every moment he stood by was a moment his mate . . . *his mate* . . . The smell. It lingered in the air again, teasing at his nostrils. The woman had been here. Good. He was on the right track. The king turned, following the scent toward the door. A nagging feeling pulled at him, a familiar being having been present here too. He could feel the magic. In the back of his mind he remembered that Sebastian was lost to this world as well.

The king paused, hand of the knob of the door as images flashed through his mind. Sebastian's hand lingered on his mate's hips, kissing her with his foul disgusting mouth. Fuck the Wicked Prince. His mate would have the answers he needed. His priority was her.

Vareck glamored himself and pushed open the doors, the city lights and busy streets blaring at a full speed. It was a shocking change of pace from the frozen wastelands of Faerie. Smog covered the roads as large carriages without horses zipped past. The alluring scent drove him forward to a store lit by lanterns.

He crossed the street, approaching to see an old machine sitting in the window. A circular black disk with grooves sat upon it, and four men walked across the road on a piece of paper. The human device was accompanied in the display with tiny trinkets, books, and teacups. Her scent was strong, and while it lingered, he couldn't feel his bond here.

"Does this place belong to you? Or do you visit it? Are you a huntress or a collector?" He rolled the words over in his mind, pressing his hand against the glass of the front window. Just what kind of person was his mate and what was this world that she lived in? If she wanted things, he would get them for her. Any trinket she wanted. Anything to pull a smile from her soft lips, to kiss her. Make her *his*.

Vareck clutched a hand over his heart, chest pained that she seemed to be slipping through his fingers. He moved his wrist over to his nose, the fabric securely tied around it. His pupils narrowed into slits, eyes glowing as he saw the faint remnants of her trail. What was this glowing pull he could see through his eyes? It was a magic unlike he had ever used before. Whatever it was, he knew it had to do with his bond. He had a way forward.

Continuing through the night, the king trekked on foot as he followed the fading scent of orange rinds and fresh grass. This city he wandered was quick to place other distracting and distasteful scents as he moved through the crowds. He started to feel the light tug at his heart strings. Every step guided him closer to her as he quickened his pace. A few rows of two-story dwellings lined the street, and Vareck could feel his heart pounding. She was here. She was close. The very last building near the far corner had the lights on, one of the doors open. The only barrier seemed to be an odd screen for what Vareck could only assume was filtering air.

Her scent wafted through, filling his senses and teasing him with a hunger that boiled deep within. He entered, door unlocked, to the huntress's humble abode. Tiny elephant figurines lined the front room shelf, the collection continuing into her house. Shoes strewn themselves across the mudroom, a dangerous hazard to unwanted guests. Was it a way to keep people out? Where were her maids? Vareck stepped over the mess, into the kitchen.

What he saw before him never failed to consume

every part of his being. The woman paused, piece of cloth half in a bag as her fingers swiped across some sort of human device. She was distracted. Even though her back was turned to him, the king knew it was her. Every feature of the woman now felt permanently burned into his mind. The way the light hit her seemed to shine through every bit of her perfection, even now.

His eyes bore into her as he traced each curve of her body. The way her hair sat on her shoulders, unpinned and in free-flowing bright auburn mess. Freckles continued to line her skin, even on the curve of her shoulders. He wondered where else he could find them, what parts of her body they would lead him to. The way she still wore the half-torn dress from the ball had his fingers itching to tear the article to shreds. It had happened while she was running.

Anger coursed through him, the continuous rejection settling in now that he was in her presences. Vareck was the king of the fae, and she was one of his subjects. Then again, none of his subjects cared for him as the leader of Faerie. What was one more? The thought ran bitter through his mind.

The king's teeth gritted together, moving forward with the grace of a predator sneaking in on their prey. Counting down from three, he acted. A hand pressed over the woman's mouth as he held her tightly against him. He didn't trust her not to pull another trick from up her sleeve. He couldn't take his eyes off her for more than one reason. Earlier, she had proved to be both crafty and powerful. He never had anyone dominate him with their persuasion before and he wouldn't let it happen again.

She immediately struggled against his grasp, shoulders thrashing as the device fell to the ground. His mate was certainly a woman who wouldn't go down without a fight. While he respected that vigor, he was done with this game. He leaned forward, the emotion of the last few hours ringing through him as he let out a ragged breath. "You don't get to run from me."

The device the woman had been tinkering with buzzed against the hardwood floor, rotating as the screen lit up. The fae screamed into his hand; the noise muffled with his palm. It took a long while of Vareck's patience, but he didn't mind standing there, holding her too him. Now that he had found her, there was all the time in the world for her to tire out. The woman paused in her fight, breathing heavily through her nose. It was then that he decided to move.

The king shifted his free hand onto her pale, creamy thigh. His fingers trailed up the side, sliding against her smooth skin. It felt odd compared to his rough, calloused hand. He had to restrain himself from exploring every part of her. The action caused the woman to stiffen, and he almost wished he could see her face. Gazing up, he was granted what he requested. The two partially had their reflections skewed back to them in an old, antique, silver-plated vase.

"I just want to ensure there are no more . . . surprises." His fingers grabbed hold to the dagger on her thigh, unleashing it from its casing. He flipped the blade over in his hand, admiring it before bringing the blade back over his shoulder. His arm extends forward with a snap, the dagger sticking into the wall ahead of them.

The fae in his arms huffed through the gag, turning her face to look up at him with a glare. She had so many looks that were still impossible to decipher. Was she particularly fond of that wall he just assaulted? Regardless, it would best to leave as quickly as possible.

"Stay still. Don't speak," he commanded, eyes glowing as he bore into her. The woman silently snarled as he removed his hold. Vareck was pleased to see that the order had taken. Leaning down to shuffle through the bag's contents, he picked out a few things he needed. "Open your mouth, do not speak," he directed, and the woman begrudgingly followed. She tried to take a step back, breaking through on his first command as she fought not to open her mouth for him.

He grabbed her by the waist, bringing her back as he placed the sock in her mouth, closing her jaw. The woman gaged, but he was quick to tape across her mouth, getting to work on tying together her legs and arms with rope. Each step of the way the huntress fought against him, as wild as a mare in spring. But all creatures can be broken, and he could tell she was losing steam.

With his work finished, he stood back to admire the final product. She looked absolutely pissed. He crossed his arms scratching his chin as she pulled against the items that bound her.

"Alright, that's out of the way. Now, how do we get you back?" he contemplated aloud. She rolled her eyes at the king. She was being incredibly judgmental for a woman who had the time to plan out her whole scheme. Vareck had acted, for the first time in a long while, without thinking everything through. He hadn't exactly ever jumped into this human world before, and it's not like he had time to plan.

Vareck leaned down to the girl bound together on the floor. He placed a hand under her chin, forcing her gaze up. "You were quite impressive earlier. I would not have to tie you up if I could trust you. Your persuasions are quite strong; remarkably so."

She jerked her face away from him, straining once more against the rope. Her brows furrowed, glare cutting in deep as she let out a frustrated, muffled scream. Vareck sighed. "If I let you go, would you be willing to cooperate?"

The woman paused, looking up with an odd gaze. She looked at him as if he had a horn in the middle of his forehead. While her hands were tied, she could still move her fingers. Both middle ones shot up in Vareck's direction. The king chuckled; voice low as he shook his head. "That answers that question," he mused.

He leaned over her body, getting a tight grip on her as he picked her up. With little effort, he managed to toss her over his shoulder like a sack of flour. The woman tried to scream out once more, squirming against his hold. Vareck held onto her as she moved and wiggled, leaning against the wall as she struggled with all her might. The man bit down on his lower lip, eyes gleaming over with a slight haze as she moved.

"Stop," he whispered under his breath. It was sort of sick. He shouldn't be so aroused by his mate being tied up, rubbing against him. But it was the silk of her ripped dress, creeping up her legs as she unmeaningly created friction. Regardless of anything else, it would be inappropriate to claim her without her consent. She was his mate. He would protect her . . . as soon as she quit being stubborn.

Vareck let out a soft groan, feeling the heated blood in his veins travel downward. He would do anything right now to go feral, to act on instinct. If only he could grind back down against her and make her feel good. Please her in a way only he knew he could. "Stop . . . stop moving. You are going to hurt yourself," he growled, the words not a command but a request. Did she notice the hard-on she was giving him? Royal wear felt far too tight for this occasion.

She either didn't care, didn't notice, or continued to be one of the most obnoxiously stubborn creatures he had ever encountered. The buzzing noise continued once more, the girl seeming to double her efforts from the commotion. He turned to face the flat, glowing object. Two females appeared on the screen as it buzzed, his mate and another female. They were both laughing, bright blue ocean water behind them. The ocean? Had she seen it?

The trail of thought reminded him of the hellscape in which they were to return. He frowned as he crushed the flat device and a satisfying crush gave way underneath his boot. Whatever the device was, it was destroyed now. The woman let out a mournful cry, doubling her efforts. Vareck sighed.

"Go to sleep," he commanded softly, the words barely loud enough for her to hear. Her struggling slowed as she fought against the suggestion, pulling against his will. Once, twice, three times she gave a final twist, slumping down to rest peacefully against him as her eyes closed and heart rate dropped. Fast asleep, Vareck moved with the woman on his shoulder through the front door.

MARA

❄

If Mara had perished during the night, she decided she was in heaven. She floated, resting on a soft, airy cloud. Everything felt warm, the woman nuzzling her cheek into whatever bliss wrapped around her skin . A few moments later she moved again, feeling the need to turn her head. Mara cracked her neck to the side, skull rolling against the doughy nirvana that lay underneath her. While most of her muscles ached, she was so thankful for her soft mattress. Wait. What?

Her eyes slowly flitted open, dazed as the ceiling blurred in and out of vision. Old Bessie, her beloved futon of four years, was anything but comfortable. While she had a bed at home, the futon was all she slept on. Her mattress was even more of a lump. But this? This wasn't hers. Had she gone to the bar last night?

Mara found it hard to focus on the day before. All

the pieces swirled around her brain in scattered, unrelated segments. There was wine, yes. Someone's lips on her own. Music that pulsed through her veins. An electricity that buzzed beneath her skin . . . The only thing that seemed to hurt besides her stiff joints was the burn around her wrists. There was also this odd pressure on her legs that made her shins ache. Too much dancing?

She groaned, squinting at the light that reflected off the pale blue ceiling. If she had been drinking before, she was unmistakably dehydrated now. Did it matter whose bed she shared when it was this comfortable? Mara would stay here forever if she could. The lull of sleep was quick to tempt her once more and she went to roll on her side.

But she couldn't. Her hands wouldn't separate. Mara's eyes snapped open, bringing her bound wrists to her face. Oh no. No. No. No. The fae shot up, letting out a muffled groan. Every part of the world spun around in circles, her body punishing her for breaking her equilibrium so quickly.

"Always the moment he walks out. I called it. Told him it would happen," a voice grumbled from near her legs. Mara's vision slowly cleared to reveal a large cat settled upon them. His head turned to the side, right ear twitching back as he examined her. What kind of cat could even be that big besides a Maine Coon? He stretched his paws out in front of him, yawning as Mara sized him up. His fur was gray with black patterned lines that covered his body. Darker patches outlined his gaze like eyeliner, and his coat seemed exceptionally well-groomed.

The bright, violet eyes of the cat scanned the woman curiously. The feline was unlike any Mara had ever seen. She always assumed she was a dog person, but this big guy was cute. His tail slowly twitched, moving from side to side. "Fine, I guess I'll just handle everything myself. Like always." The cat sighed, bringing his paw up to his face with a few licks. Mara froze at a realization. The voice from earlier had come from the cat. The cat spoke in an archaic version of ancient fae and what's worse was that she understood him. "So . . . uh, how are you feeling?"

The cat. The cat was talking to her. The cat asked her a question.

Her head snapped to one edge of the room, then the next. A fireplace, a reading nook, desk corner—none of it was remotely familiar. She was in a large bed with gray, fur-covered sheets. Each corner of the bed held four posts, carved in a familiar style she couldn't place. A large, draping canopy veiled over the edges of the frame, tied at the sides to allow free movement around the bed.

This was too weird. What had happened last night? *Think, Mara.* She glanced down at her dress, images of the ball slowly coming to mind. Then there was the chase, but she got back to the fountain. She left the prince at the bar, went home to pack, then texted Sadie. At the mention of her sister, memories of the night before flooded her mind. The text being interrupted by a cold, familiar voice.

Mara's hand slowly moved up to her lips, fingers stopping to feel the tape replaced by a softer fabric she didn't realize was even there. The huntress screamed into the gag, flailing with her feet to get out of the bed. She scooted herself to the side, feeling the weight leave her legs as she neared the edge. Her foot caught on one of the blankets, Mara tumbling out with a heavy groan. Her dress hiked up over her hips as the blanket still wrapped around her left leg, most of the covers still in the bed. Laying there on the ground, Mara sighed deeply.

"She is beauty, she is grace." A small shadow hovered over her as the bedroom door opened. The cat settled onto the corner of the bed, ears flattening at her new position. He turned to see his master standing by the door, looking rightfully confused. "Real catch you've got here."

The king closed the door before rushing over to check on the her, shooing the cat away from her. Mara began to panic the moment the Winter King was in her sights. Every memory rushed into her mind of him tying her up and commanding her to comply. She sat up quickly, struggling against the bonds as she tried to give him a piece of her mind. All the words were distorted and incomprehensible beneath the gag. He shook his head, icy blue gaze giving her a sympathetic look. The king reached out, hands moving towards her.

Oh no, none of that again! The last time Mara was in the king's arms she woke up in this place. The woman dug her heel into the carpet pushing back with all her might. She thrashed around, desperate to free her leg from the mess of fur that waterfalled off the side of the bed. The king quirked a brow, watching her as she scrambled into the corner of the room.

He shook his head. "I'm trying to help you." A small huff left hip lips. "You are going to have to get used to me touching you, Huntress."

Touching her? Mara absorbed the thought, staring as she inwardly fought the statement. She remembered the way his hand had moved up her thigh. Every touch from him felt electric. Not to mention he could pick her up and carry her over his muscled shoulder like nothing. The woman shook her head, trying to clear the odd but alluring temptations. How was it that she was still attracted to this monster?

The king held up his hands, palms flat in a show of peace, slowly moving forward. She waited, watching him silently as he moved. Once the king was close enough, she shot out her leg, kicking him. Mara landed a harsh blow to his arm, smirking through the gag. From the corner of her vision, she saw a gray mass move across the back of the room. The cat that had tried to talk to her before jumped up onto one of the shelves of books. While his front paws found purchase, the rest of him scrambled to properly sit on the top ledge.

The king took this distraction, moving in once more. This time when she kicked, he caught her foot. His brow raised as he pulled her legs apart, Mara looking up at him in horror. Maybe it wasn't the best idea to press herself into the corner. How could she possibly escape this?

With her legs spread, the king moved in between them, hovering over her. He leaned in, voice low as he whispered, "If you did not fight me at every turn, I may be inclined to remove the gag." His voice trailed off, letting the offer float between them. While Mara felt more than uneasy about the whole situation, she slowly let the tension of her body go. She swallowed dryly, glancing to the side. She couldn't even bear to look at him.

"Good girl," he said. Remembering her own words when she had commanded him the night before, she glared at him. He shot a small wink, readjusting his position and Mara rolled her eyes. So close in proximity, she watched the way he looked at her. Was he . . . smelling her? He leaned in, mouth hovering over her neck before placing a soft kiss.

Mara inwardly cursed herself for enjoying the touch, neck tilting towards the side as a strand of her hair fell in front of her face. Everything about this was wrong. She wanted nothing to do with the this fae, right? His mouth moved up from the crook of her neck, tongue trailing against her skin. He continued his journey up, breath fanning over the tip of her ear. Electricity inflamed her nerves with every touch, chills running up her spine.

Focus, Mara. Can you get your shit together, girl?

She couldn't lose sight of everything now. This maniac king had just abducted her. Did he think she was just going to lie down and take it? It seemed that he knew little to nothing about her. Good. Let him underestimate what she was capable of.

The determination wavered once more at the next kiss. His lips pressed beneath her ear, leaving a trail down the line of her jaw. One after the other they peppered her skin. Mara's shoulder rolled, turning her face compliantly towards him with his touch, her body screaming for the attention, her mind fighting for control. His mouth lingered below the edges of the rag, skimming over the top of her lips. No. No way.

Mara snarled; head rearing back. She flung her head forward, knocking his skull with whatever force she could find. Quiet curses left the kings lips as he fell back, Mara ignoring the pain in her face to scramble up and sprint out of the corner. Blood dripped from the king's hand as he looked between her and his palm in shock. She didn't take the time to wait, rushing towards the door.

"Well, would you look at that. You've got your work cut out, V," the cat mused, watching her from the safety of his shelf. *It's a cat . . . what in the actual hell . . .*

While her hands were still tied together it wouldn't

stop her. She'd get out of here even if it killed her. Mara grabbed onto the handle of the door, pausing in fear at a loud knock.

"King Vareck?" a female voice called out, knocking a second time. "Are you present? Dorian informed me that you've returned."

Mara shot back a few steps, adrenaline the only thing to keep her on her feet. How could she possibly run from the king and all his staff? If it was a maid, perhaps. But this didn't sound like a maid. She was screwed. Her eyes widened, panic spreading as she crossed more and more options. She couldn't use her magic, nobody knew where she was, and her hands were bound. Mara found it hard to breathe, and it had nothing to do with the gag in place. Her chest heaved, eyes scanning the room for anything she could find useful. Back and forth her focus turned from Vareck to the door as he stood.

The window. How high was she off the ground? What was underneath? Whether it was soft snow, or jagged rocks Mara didn't have time to mull over the decision. One thing was clear. If she stayed with the Winter King, she would die. He took her from her home and now he was holding her hostage for what she had done to the prince. She didn't want to think about how much he would torture her or use her for his pleasure. It was far better to die on her own terms than live like that.

"V, promise me you didn't bring home someone as

unstable as you," the cat's ears flattened, looking like he'd just figured out what she was thinking. Mara sprinted forward, turning her shoulder towards the window.

"Oh, great. She's worse!" the cat hissed, tail standing up straight.

The glass shattered around her and the bite of winter enveloped her skin as she burst forth into the icy storm.

VARECK

❄

The fight boiling beneath the surface of the huntress was never unsurprising. Vareck hissed as he gingerly held onto his nose. Having her beneath him . . . her scent was so powerful. The previously enticing aromas of his mate were now replaced with pain and iron. For a smaller woman, her attacks seemed to hurt him the most. You would think that the stab from the night before had been worse. But the magic that healed and repaired his body always drained him of his resources, and this would take more time as a result.

Bloodied and dripping, the king covered his nose with his palm. He sat back, somewhat dazed by the unexpected attack. What was that for? She had seemed to be enjoying herself.

"V, promise me you didn't bring home someone as unstable as you," his companion called out, the cat's voice the first thing to reach him. He glanced over just in time to see his mate looking around wildly like a captive animal. Vareck noted that the more he pressed, the harder she fought back.

The huntress was a warrior, true to her red-headed nature. Fiery, passionate, and . . . looking at the window? No . . . she wouldn't. He inhaled sharply as the he watched her decision to run.

"NO!" he cried out, reaching his hand towards her. Even with his magic, however, her momentum was already in place. Her body hit the window, glass shattering as the cold winds of winter pierced the room. The door to the quarters flew open as Vareck rushed to the window.

Down below, through the wisps of snow, Vareck watched with this breath caught in his throat. The huntress managed to land on the balls of her feet, moving the impact through a roll as she found her balance. She looked back up to the window, her wide eyes meeting his gaze before taking off. Not hesitating for even a moment, she broke off into a sprint across the first-floor roof. The woman ran from him again. Whatever worry that had burrowed itself into his chest at her daring the jump quickly dissipated. Now it was replaced with fury. He could feel the anger course through him as his nails extended to talons, his body shaking from trying to quell his rage. He needed to focus.

Kaia, as quick and silent as ever, approached the king's side. "Vareck, what just happened?" Her hand touched his shoulder, guiding him to face her. She frowned at the drying blood that dripped from his nose. Her gaze turned out into the storm.

"Who is she?"

"My mate." The words reluctantly left his tongue, tasting bitter against his lips. "I'll be back." He sighed, pushing out the jagged glass on the frame with his palm. What a hell of a woman. How fitting that the vixen be as much of a punishment as the rest of his life. Vareck grabbed onto the window, pulling himself through as he jumped.

He landed gracefully, expression stoic as he took off after her. The bite of winter nipped at his skin, Vareck unfazed by the cold. His cloak whipped behind him as the king twisted the button at his neck. He freed the fabric, allowing it to flow into the courtyard. Within moments he caught up to the woman, an easier task to run in the snow with boots.

"You are the biggest pain I have ever met," he hissed, moving to grab the huntress around the waist. She dropped down to the ground, squatting before using her momentum to slide through his legs.

"Stop," he commanded, the woman's feet slowing in the snow. "You are going to hurt yourself, or lose a foot to frostbite if you don't get inside." She turned to look at him, and while her body shivered her eyes flared with fire. Vareck grunted, walking over and reaching down to scoop her up in his arms. One look at her caused his upper lip to involuntarily snarl. "What am I supposed to do about you, Huntress?"

Not wanting to see her cold demeanor, he tossed her back over his shoulder. The woman shrieked, pounding her tied fists against his back. Once, twice, three times before she seemed to run out of steam. The king carefully treaded against the rooftop, back to his window as he called up to his guard.

"Kaia!"

The blonde stuck her head outside the window, brow raised as she watched their interaction from afar. "If she is indeed your mate, you have an odd way of showing your bond," she called down to him as she cupped her hands around her mouth.

He glared at her. Only Kaia would dare goad him right now. He looked around the rooftop, trying to see if there was anything of use. "Can you help me get her up to the room? Throw down a rope or . . . something." He heard the cat cackle, no doubt enjoying Vareck's misery.

"Are you . . . serious right now?"

"Of course, I am. How else am I getting back up there with her?"

"Can't you just . . . jump off the roof?"

"I don't need the court to know of this, especially with her trying to run off every other minute."

Kaia drummed her fingers against her cheek, elbow sitting in the palm of her hand. "This is a horrible idea," she muttered. "Alright. Hold still."

Vareck waited, frowning as a flake dared to assault his eye. He moved his hand towards her dangling toes, trying to bring back some warmth to them as the two waited in silence. Well . . . mostly silence. The woman still seemed to curse at him through the gag.

A small while later, a rope was thrown out the window settling by the foot of the wall. Vareck got to work, quickly wrapping it around his mate before connecting it to the binds of her hands. The woman glared with the raw heat of summer every time he stole a glance. He was tired with these games, and honestly, he'd had enough. "Hey." He snapped his fingers in front of her face to get her attention. "You chose to jump. Do not be angry with me for it."

Telling someone not to be angry at him? What a useless task. He squeezed her shoulder, tilting his head to the side. "Hold tight. Not that you have a choice."

MARA

❄

Mara curled up on the bed, one of the fur blankets wrapped around her shoulders. While her body shook, she still tried to move. Repeatedly the guard he called Kaia had to command her, compelling her to stay. But she knew if she kept pushing against the guard's magic it would drain her. Keep moving. Keep resisting. Mara would make this hell for them if that's what it took to get her freedom. The king pulled himself through the window, the guard stepping back. Kaia seemed a little unsteady on her feet.

"My commands are already wearing off on her," the guard noted, taking another one of the blankets from the bed and offering it up to the king. Mara felt the order loosening, pulling herself from the comfort of the bed once more.

"Sit, would you?" the king huffed, taking the blanket from the woman. Instead of placing it on his own body he moved to drape it across Mara's shoulders. "Yes, her power is quite strong. She overpowered me with her persuasion last night. That's how she got away."

Mara huffed. She happily took the compliment but would appreciate it more if they didn't talk about her like she wasn't in front of them on the bed.

"Corvo, would you mind?" the king asked.

"On it." The cat plopped down from the shelf, tail twitching as a snowflake landed on the tip of his forehead. Corvo's violet eyes glowed effervescently, similar in the way that a fae's would when using magic. The same hue circled him, the cat turning his nose towards the window as a violet barrier covered the shattered opening. "Should last a few hours," the cat yawned, trotting off.

Mara slowly shifted her legs to the side of the bed. With the king distracted by the . . . the magic cat . . . this was her time to move. She tried to creep as quietly as possible, but there were so many blankets surrounding her body. The king instantly turned his head towards her. A frown skewed across his face as he commanded her once more. "Stay there. Rest. Get warm."

The guard sighed, pinching the bridge of her nose as she watched the back and forth between them. "How exactly do you plan on holding her here?" She shifted her hips to the side, arms crossing in front of her chest. Mara glanced over, slightly uncomfortable at the scrutinizing gaze of this woman. Was she his lover?

"That is a great question." The king let out a light sigh, pulling himself away from the fae as he headed back towards the window.

"Vareck." Mara watched as the woman named Kaia called the king by his first name, turning her head towards the deranged man. "She doesn't want to be here."

The king's mouth pressed into a thin line, holding out his hands. "What do you want me to say?"

"Well, for one thing, a solution that doesn't involve her being trussed up like a turkey." Kaia sighed, leaning her neck into the palm of her hand. Her gaze shifted between Mara, then to the King, and then back. What could she possibly be looking for? "How in the world is she your mate. We don't even have mates anymore. Ever since the—"

"I'm well aware, Kaia."

"But you're saying . . . you're saying you *feel* it? It happened? Does she know, Vareck?"

Mara's head snapped towards the guard, body freezing up colder than from the ice outside. Did she hear that right? *Mate?* Her eyes darted between Kaia and the king, shoulders dropping as she leaned back against the frame of the bed. She couldn't believe it. Mate?

"Well, she certainly does now," Corvo called out,

observing the room from the safety of the warm reading nook.

Mara's gaze settled onto the king, her body still for the first time since her morning doze. This man, the Winter King of all of Faerie, was her mate? What type of foolery was this? What type of plot or ploy? While it was true that he hadn't hurt her—or really harmed her in any way besides some partially unwanted advances and retrieval—was it alright to believe? No, it couldn't be. It would be laughable: an orphaned half fae from the human realm mated to royalty. The Winter King was said to be as cold and unforgiving as the land. Well, it's not that Mara even stayed or visited much of her homeland. The human world was often where she felt she belonged. But she couldn't help but remember the touch of his lips against her neck, the way he breathed in her scent, and looked into her eyes like he was seeing into her very core. Like he understood her in a way that she didn't even understand herself. The way his rough hands trailed up towards the apex of her thigh. *Damnit. Focus, Mara.* While she was attracted to him, not once had she felt a *bond* between her and this man.

Having and finding a mate was all anyone talked about growing up. Her parents were a bunch of love-struck fools and had ingrained the idea of having a true mate into her and Sadie the moment they'd found an interest in anyone. At twenty-five, Mara had given up on feeling the pull or connection of her "mate," and she wasn't about to start now.

Plus, instead of just talking to her about it, he'd kidnapped her. He couldn't have just talked to her like a normal person. But no. He chased her through a castle, acted crazy when he saw her, then followed her to the human world like a stalker. And here was she was. Mara let out a frustrated sigh from between the gag, her attention soon picking up on soft whispers from across the room. Had she spaced?

"Do you think the curse has finally come to an end?" Kaia whispered, her back turned from Mara.

"She is only the beginning of it." The king hadn't turned away, his arms crossed as he spoke. He clearly didn't trust Mara not to try something the moment his back was turned. His eyes met hers momentarily, soon shifting his gaze once more. "I can feel it start to unravel. It is why I need her, Kaia. Not just for me—which I do; she is my mate—but for Faerie. I owe it to my people to make things right. You said it yourself. I am not giving up."

While he wasn't facing her, Mara could see the small smile that grew on the guard's face. She could only hear snippets of the conversation, but none of it made any sense without the context. "I need to talk to her without the risk of being persuaded. Any ideas?"

"Not the slightest," Kaia mused, turning to face Mara as well.

"Corvo?" the king tried prompting the curled-up cat to be of some sort of use in the conversation.

"I'm tired; leave me alone."

"Corvo, I—"

"Sorry, V. Not my area of expertise." The cat yawned, tucking his head in on his body.

"That cat is useless." The king sighed. "There must be another way."

A soft hum rolled from Kaia's lips, "Perhaps." Her light blue eyes returned to face Mara, giving the woman a small smile. Mara couldn't help but glance away, a pressure of some unknown task setting deep into her gut. "Perhaps not. Give it your best try. I'll try to dig something up in the meantime."

"Very well, see if Lorne or any of the healers have anything to note on the topic. But don't mention why."

"As you wish." Kaia placed her left hand in front of her chest, giving the king a deep bow. She turned to leave, head pausing to take one final look at Mara. She didn't need to speak, Mara practically hearing her thoughts.

Silence settled with just the two of them left lingering in the room. Well, the two of them and that cat. Corvo didn't seem to want anything to do with them, ears occasionally twitching as he napped. The king took a step towards the corner of the bed, sitting on the edge. His mouth opened, lips making odd shapes as he figured out how to start. He seemed to give up, moving his fingertips to knead into the back of his neck.

So, this was Vareck Blackthorne, the Winter King. With the new opportunity to sit in silence with him, Mara observed his habits . . . and his assets. A small crease settled into his brow as he thought; his gray-blue eyes as cold as the ice itself. He had gazed her over with a wild look before, but now that it was just them, he didn't seem able to keep his attention steady. Slight dark circles edged around the bottom of his eyes, and besides the newly healing nose, he was quite handsome. His shoulders and arms were heavily muscled, and she admired the V shape of his upper body. He appeared defeated right now, and even then he was regal and intimidating. His hair was a chestnut brown, wild and unruly. His jawline was sharp enough to shank someone. A blush rose to her cheeks, quickly dismissing it, telling herself they were important things to know. She snorted in derision. *Yeah, important if I was drawing him. His jawline won't find me any ways out of here.*

Mara's deep dive and admiration into Vareck's looks were interrupted with a loud, groaning growl of her stomach. It was noisy enough for the king to hear, the man quirking a brow and letting loose a huff of a laugh. The woman straightened in her place, squinting her eyes at him. It wasn't her fault that the only thing in her stomach was alcohol and a peanut butter sandwich. Come to think of it, that was the night before—

"My apologies, you are probably starving," he chatted quietly to Mara as if she could reply, the woman quirking her brow. What was he going to do, feed her applesauce around the gag? No, thank you.

"Corvo, see to it that the attendants bring lunch for her."

"Seriously? Six seconds is not a cat nap, V."

"Yes, seriously. I need your help."

Corvo appeared to contemplate the request, begrudgingly pulling himself up from his spot. "Alright. But not for you. For the girl. She's crazy; I like her." She watched as Corvo hopped down, lazily waddling towards the door.

Vareck turned to Mara. "Well, it seems you have a fan."

"All mighty powerful god, to cat, to food server. I'm moving up, baby," Corvo called over his shoulder, trotting out of the room.

Vareck pinched the bridge of his nose. "Sorry about him. He is a little . . . catty."

Corvo peered his head back inside, glaring up at his master. "I *heard* that, and you should be ashamed."

"Corvo."

"Right, right; the food. Don't talk about me while I'm gone."

Vareck slowly turned back to her as she sat tied up in front of him and he appeared to be weighing his options. She watched him curiously as he took a deep breath, looking into her eyes as his pupils turned to slits, an icy blue glow radiating out into the room. "I'm going to remove the gag. Do not persuade me or use any of your magic against me. Do not attack me in any form. Do not break my nose, stab me, or run from me. Again."

Third times the charm, right?

Vareck shifted from the foot of the bed, sliding up to sit next to her. His hands moved to the back of her head, untying the fabric that barred her from speaking.

Mara didn't say a word at first, gazing over at him as if he would attack her at any moment. She watched with wide eyes, rubbing at the raw corners of her mouth. Of all things that were certain, Mara was beyond pleased to have the pressure away from her face. To move her mouth and speak was something she had always taken for granted. She needed to turn the tables on this whole being held captive thing.

"What's your name?" he asked.

Mara should have been prepared to speak now that she was on the king's agenda. But now that he wanted her to talk, why should she? Being his "mate" didn't give him any right to kidnap her. Her words would only be given when he earned them.

"Answer me, honestly," the king command, another glow to his gaze.

"Mara." The word was pulled from her tongue like a sigh, the woman glancing to the side as she was forced to answer. Guess he got what he wished for after all. What a nuisance to be persuaded for such useless information. "Mara Wylde."

"Mara," he repeated. "Mara, it is. My name is Vareck Blackthorne. Which I suppose you already know."

She stared about him pointedly. Of course. He was the king of the fae realm. Did he think she was dense?

The king smoothed out one of the fur blankets, contemplating the next question to ask. "Who are you? Who are you working for?"

"No one. No one, really. Myself." That much was true, at least in Mara's mind. "I'm a collector and an anthropologist . . . of sorts. I find items—artifacts— and on occasion, people. If the price is right." Oh, how the price for the Wicked Prince was wrong.

"How have you managed to make your persuasion as powerful as it is?"

"I . . . I don't know." Her voice turned small, slowly moving to finally meet his gaze. "There's a lot I don't know about myself."

"Well, what are you? Do you know that?"

"Rude, and still no. Probably half high fae and maybe redcap? I dunno."

"What about your powers? What can you do?"

"You ask too many questions, you know that?" she grumbled, feeling the pull that would make her answer and making her groan. "I can find things. Or people. I just need to see it once, and there you go: found. Beyond my persuasion being strong enough to subdue *you*, that is" she said with a smirk. She heard a rumble in his chest, no doubt recalling her controlling him. She imagined he liked to be the one in control.

"Yes, we've established that. Do you have an affinity? A familiar, perhaps?"

"I don't, actually."

"My affinity is spirit. Corvo is my familiar, though he's also a pain in my ass as you can tell."

The door to the room opened, abruptly ending their conversation, a tray hovering in the air as an ethereal hand lingered in behind the cat. The mostly unseen servant set the tray down on the bed in front of the king, giving a small dip of a flourish.

"Thank you, Charles." The hand bowed once again before seeing itself out. Mara watched with wide eyes.

"What the fuck was that?"

"Rude," he mused, using her earlier tone. "He was one of my servants, and a great man."

"*He?* It was just a *hand*!"

"For having such an interested eye for items, it appears that there is a lot you fail to see," he chuckled, taking the soup off the tray. "Are you hungry?"

Mara was quiet for a moment, contemplating an answer. "Are you going to command me to tell you?"

Vareck grabbed for a spoon, pausing in his work. "If you are going to be stubborn, I will."

"Fine. I'm starving," Mara said, biting her bottom lip. Vareck seemed somewhat pleased at her voluntary openness, but the man should know better. This was clearly all for the food. Vareck scooped up a half spoonful of the reddish-brown soup. The smell of squash and cinnamon wafted through the air as he cooled it with his breath.

He gazed up at her, blowing on it once more before he trailed the spoon over to her lips. His hand sat beneath the utensil, ready to catch whatever dropped so it didn't burn her. Mara watched, a little dazed when the spoon approached her. Of course, she had eaten soup before, but never in her life had she been fed by another.

Feeling slightly intimidated by it all, it took Mara a moment to open her mouth. That half bite was all Mara needed to instantly want more. The warmth from the creamy broth radiated down to her toes, surely enchanted with different types of warming spices. The deep chill from the frost that had once ailed her was no more.

Vareck fed her another, then the next, each one Mara hesitating before chomping down. She missed the third bite, getting a little on the corner of her mouth. The king moved in closer, dabbing a napkin to clean up the light mess. Mara would rather die than admit how nice it was to have someone else taking care of her.

"Have you always lived in the human world?"

"As far as I remember." He fed her another bite for the answer. She saw his eyes lose focus for a moment.

Using his magic to keep her in place was likely more tiresome than he had ever imagined and that made her smile inside.

"How did you end up here?"

"A contract." Another spoonful. It was almost like a game, Vareck handing out questions as he desperately searched for answers while Mara vaguely answered them to the best of her ability.

"Did you not know I was your mate?" Vareck asked.

Mara frowned, gaze turning down to her bound hands. "No . . ." Her own eyes flickered their vibrant green hue. "Am I actually your mate?"

"Yes, of course."

"Would you release me?"

Vareck's expression was stoic as he narrowed his eyes at her. She was testing the waters and went too far; he must have felt it. The king grabbed the gag, Mara gasping as she tried to move away. Damnit! She tried to escape, but he already had her pinned, quickly putting the gag back in place.

"Nice try. This was fun," Vareck said dryly as she simmered below the surface. The king grabbed one of the winter apple slices from the plate, taking a bite with a smirk.

KAIA

There was only one lead Kaia had to work off of. And while it wasn't a main priority to the king at the moment, Sebastian needed to be found as well. Yes, Vareck's focus seemed to solely revolve around the fae with red hair, apparently named Mara. If it wasn't for the current state of the realm, Kaia would inwardly mark this obsession as excessive. But to be fair, she didn't know the pull of the mate bond. Unless they were already bonded before . . . no one did.

Which is why the right-hand of the king found herself stepping into the human realm. A neon sign glowed up ahead, pink cursive words with a sparkle after them humming in the night. The Witching Hour had been the only reliable source to go off of thus far, the name itself coming from the king's lips.

To be honest, she had hardly ever stepped foot into the human realm. As one of the king's guard, she never really had the need to leave Vareck's side. But for him and his new mate, finding answers was the most essential thing to the kingdom and the curse that lingered over the land.

The blonde fae stepped through the entrance of the nightclub, pushing the doors aside. The fountain portal had been disenchanted the moment the King had returned to the realm. Kaia had to give the little bounty hunter points for turning such a mundane object into her escape route. The protection of the magic had always been focused inside of the castle, and not the grounds themselves. Magic itself was unwieldy, and the guards couldn't possibly predict and protect the king from every fountain and tree that turned into a port.

Focused on the task at hand, Kaia moved through the crowd. Her dark green dress hugged her body, straps settled onto both of her shoulders. Her waist cinched inward with a black, leather bodice, laced up each of the sides. Hunting boots crawled up to her thighs, allowing comfort as she walked. The outfit was readily able to fit in while still allowing her to take down anyone she needed to.

Kaia was here on business, not pleasure. She approached the bar, sitting down in front of the barkeep. The witch behind the counter was burrowed into black furs, a royal purple streak running across her face in a single line through her eyes. The witch was in the middle of a performance, singing a song as patrons hit their mugs against the bar.

She cackled, bowing deeply to her audience as they cheered, the woman shouting, "Another round on the house!" A resounding chorus of agreements filled the room, men clanking their drinks together as bottles flew to fill cups. The barkeep laughed, settling herself in front of Kaia.

"Welcome, welcome to my hour. The hour is me. How can I entertain you?" the witch cooed.

Kaia was taken aback, not expecting such a strong entrance from the other woman. "I'm on a search. I was told you could help me."

"People say a lot of things these days. Not everything you hear is true." The witch pulled up a seat on her side of the bar, sitting across from Kaia with her hands in her lap. "How about a drink and then we talk shop?"

"Oh, no, I don't partake—"

"Nonsense. You need to drink to live," she insisted, sitting back as she surveyed Kaia. "I think you're a tea kind of gal, yes? Green?"

Kaia blinked, allowing for a small smile. "Black."

"Daring. I like you," the witch teased, rolling her wrist in a circle. Cups floated down from a cabinet on the side wall, saucers sliding across the bar. Kaia grabbed for the dagger at her side, jolting at the noise.

She chuckled. "All is well, Guardian. It's just our brew." Long delicate fingers picked up the kettle acquired from underneath the bar, pouring the hot water over loose leaves. Finally, she threw down a bottle of bourbon, topping off just her cup. "Cheers to a new friendship. I'm Amelia. Tell me who you are, and who or what of yours needs finding."

Kaia paused, moving her hand away from the dagger to pick up the delicate cup. "One request at a time, I suppose." She understood the king's priorities. And once Vareck's mate was under control, she could find out where Mara took Sebastian. "My name is Kaia, and you apparently already know who I am."

"I know the look of the king's guards. You all have that thing about you. Hard to describe, but easy to see." Amelia winked at her. "But you don't often leave Faerie and join us here. Did you bring the handsome warrior? The one with the tattoos that's always scowling?" she asked, looking around behind Kaia.

"Dorian?"

"That's the one."

Kaia was taken by surprise and wasn't sure how to respond. "How do you know Dorian?" she said skeptically.

Amelia's eyes sparkled. "Better question: who don't I know? Now about that other question"—she waved her hand to continue the conversation as though they were old friends—"who or what of yours needs finding?"

She stumbled on her words. "I, uh . . . I'm in need of an artifact, or a spell. Something that can dampen, hold, or absorb the power of a very strong fae. That would preferably not be permanent."

Hopefully one day Mara would trust and work alongside the rest of them. She couldn't blame the woman for her current resentment. It had been days and the king had seemed to make little to no progress with the tied-up girl.

"An artifact or spell, eh?" Amelia brought the teacup to her lips, sipping it with a small sigh. Kaia subtly waved her fingers over her own cup, checking it for poison or enchantment. Finding it clear, she gently blew on the scalding hot liquid before taking her own sip as the witch contemplated.

Amelia's fingers tapped on her chin. "Personally, I do not. However, I have a few connections that are willing to dig up anything for the right amount. Come back at this time tomorrow. I'll know whether or not my contacts know of anything of the sort. You may just be in luck."

A return visit? Kaia inwardly tensed at the idea of having to come back to the loud, stuffed club once again. Still, with no other leads to go on, this was as good as it was going to get.

"Thanks for the tea."

"My absolute pleasure, Kaia."

She got up to walk away and she couldn't help but turn around and steal another glance at the odd witch.

VARECK

DAYS HAD PASSED. *Days*. And still Mara resented him. The pair had at least gotten into a set routine. She would start the day by waking up and making life an absolute living hell for Vareck.

He had to keep her on watch or tied partially to the bed. It was impossible to trust her after the stunt with the window. The once beautiful stained glass was temporarily boarded up. Light emitted into the room from higher up and places with thicker panes.

The most difficult task by far, and the one that held the most space for progress, was feeding time. While the woman needed to eat, she would push it off until absolutely necessary. Then, even in her weakest state, she would consume by his hand and play along until trying to command him again. Every time. The task served to keep her alive and drew answers, but even after fifteen minutes he was exhausted. She would constantly push him far into the reserves of his magic just so he could keep hold of her.

All of his hopes were with Kaia. The rare moments Vareck had to himself were spent doing his own research on artifacts in the royal library. So far, it was all to no avail. Kaia lacked answers regardless of how much she looked. Vareck sighed, leaning over his desk as his quill scribbled across the page wildly. Oh, not to mention, he still had a cursed kingdom.

"Hey, V. Just want to put it out there," the feline began, stretching out on the side of the desk, "but that smell is definitely not my litterbox."

Vareck's pen stilled for a moment, otherwise ignoring his familiar. He finished up the line, dropping the quill back into the well of ink. He folded up the paper, heating a black stick of wax above the flame of a candle. "I am aware. Mara refuses to let me bathe her and I cannot trust her out of my sights."

"I could watch her," the cat purred, tail flicking in amusement. Corvo laughed at the almost aggressive glance he received from the king. "Relax, I'm teasing. Kind of. Sort of. I mean, I'm a cat . . . but seriously, what's the plan? Let her stink up the whole castle?"

Mara let out a loud, muffled huff from the other side of the room. Her eyes narrowed in on the cat. Corvo's tail simply curled, lowering his chin to rest back on the desk. The room was as stale as their predicament. Vareck would just need to keep searching.

The king let the wax drip onto the letter, pulling out a seal from his desk. He pressed his insignia into the molten liquid just as there was a knock on the door.

"It's Kaia, Your Grace," a voice called from the other side.

"Come in, quickly," Vareck said, his spirits lifting at the sound of her voice.

"My king," the woman bowed, her long braid draped over her shoulder.

"Stop with the formalities, Kaia. It's just us. Do you have news?" Vareck asked feverishly.

"Just the start of something, but yes," Kaia answered carefully, hands gathered in front of her. She turned slightly to the bed, giving a small nod of acknowledgement to Mara. "Good afternoon, Mara."

"What have you found?" he pressed once more, desperate for some inkling of reprieve.

"I do not know much about it yet. But I have a lead. I'm meeting a contact again tomorrow in the human realm. They'll have definitive answers for me then." Kaia bit her bottom lip as Vareck's shoulders seemed to stiffen.

"Good. Get it done," Vareck stressed. "Whatever you need to do. Do it."

Kaia placed her left fist over her chest, giving the king a solid nod. "A solution will be found, Vareck." Vareck didn't mean to push Kaia over something that initially seemed so selfish, but this was beyond him. It was for his mate. It was for his realm.

The guard stood in silence as she watched him, her arms slowly crossed, gentle in her tone. She dared to glance once more at Mara before asking, "How are things on your end?"

Corvo scoffed, turning his head away from the trio and muttered, "Well, he took her captive and professed his eternal love, so . . ."

Vareck's expression soured at his familiar's feedback, moving to slump into his desk chair. "As good as one would expect with my mild nature and deep emotional understanding. Which is to say . . . horribly."

"Your insight and yet lack of change is astonishing," Kaia mused, tilting her hip to the side. "Glad to see you can joke about it."

"I have to. The moment she is ungagged she pushes my limits. If I make one wrong move, she is gone. And she knows it." Vareck turned to face Mara, the woman already staring him down.

Kaia's smile slowly dropped, watching the frustration grow through the creases on the king's face. "Vareck. It will happen. Give it time."

Her words echoed through the now silent room, Vareck leaning back on the desk chair. He closed off at the comment, nodding his head slowly as he stared towards the decorative rug.

"It will."

"Tomorrow shall be met with better spirits. I'll report back with my findings and we'll have a place to start."

He gave a small nod, taking in a deep breath. "Yes, I suppose you have a point."

"Get some rest, Your Grace."

"Pleasant dreams, Kaia."

The guard bowed once more, stealing a final glance at Mara before slipping out the door. The silence continued its trend, Vareck watching as Mara turned her attention from the exiting guard back to him. For how long would this go on?

He pushed himself out of the desk chair, pausing to stand. Both of his fists curled, knuckles resting down on the desk as his support. Vareck gave Mara a long, long look, etching every detail of the woman into his mind for the one hundredth time.

"You surely are my salvation and my punishment." He moved from the desk, sauntering over towards the side of the bed. He took his time, sitting slowly before grabbing Mara's chin and forcing her to face him. No matter her glare, his words did not waver.

"You hate me right now. Do not worry, that message was made clear." His free hand moved to the top of her head, carding his fingers through her beautiful, tangled red hair.

He smiled, but he felt an anger boiling deep in his gut. "I'll change that." His thumb moved across her lower cheek. "You will love me. I'll make it so."

"Um, V . . ." Corvo slowly peeked his head up from his spot on the desk, earns flattening back. "I don't think it works like that."

LOU

Smoke curled around Lou's lips as he sighed, leaning back into plush cushions. The Witching Hour sure knew how to make a fae comfortable. The Black Lounge was his preferred place to operate. The underbelly of the human world was where a shifty leprechaun like Lou flourished.

The creatures here weren't ruled by royalty or class barriers. No, the driving force in this world was necessity. And with Lou happening to be the lead supplier, well . . . all hail the king. When it came to ancient artifacts, cursed scrolls, and copious amounts of illegal glamor, he owned the underground empire. His connections reached out like a spiderweb, intricately weaving everyone together in owed favors and good fortunes.

Lou's gaze flitted over to the pocket watch in his hand, huffing on his pipe before setting it down on the table. While it was close to the time he would meet his client, Lou couldn't help but resent the fact he was here to begin with.

"Amelia, I says"—Lou turned towards his bodyguard, the ash from the pipe dumping out into the tray. He slid a small box out from his pocket, a simple jewel embedded in the front. Opening the clasp revealed a mix of dried lavender and tobacco leaves—"I'm a busy, busy man. But no. She keeps throwing these saps my way."

He sighed, shaking his head as his nimble fingers packed the bowl. "I've got places to be, Frank. Items to sell. Money to find." He tapped the pipe on the table, offering it up to his guard. The half-orc shook his head, Lou shrugging before searching for his lighter.

"Aw, bugger," he cursed, tapping on his many pockets and coming up empty-handed. He soon gave in, snapping his fingers a few times instead until a small spark emitted. The lavender caught hold, curling inward as it burned. "As I was sayin', Amelia said I might be interested. I should hear this fae out." He shook his head. "The witch has a pure heart for all the darkness that surrounds her, aye. Never could say no to a pretty face."

The leprechaun's lips curved up into a smirk. "My biggest weakness is a beautiful woman, but some man has to handle all of these girls. Am I right, Frank?"

The half-orc nodded, rubbing at one of his tusks.

Lou glanced down at the pocket watch in his

hands. The ornate, golden piece hooked onto the inside of his jacket. Flipping it open indicated the time, while the other side was enchanted to show a small animation of the current weather along with any reminders from the day. It was a small trinket that the he'd found for himself amongst Mara's knickknacks.

She had seemed quite cross with him in their last encounter. Lou contemplated as the minutes went by if he should be worried by her idle threats. Nah. Mara the Mighty was a woman not motivated by money, only that she was in desperate need of it. As long as he kept her luck at bay, there was nothing to be concerned about. She'd always come back to him.

Focusing back on the client that would shortly be arriving, Lou snapped the watch closed one more. Amelia hadn't said too much about this new blood besides the lass looked like a high fae in search of a something special. Whoever it was, he hoped their pockets were as deep as their status.

An artifact that can cancel out another's powers. He already had what the woman needed. A ring of nullification? A cursed item like that was surprisingly common. A single prick from one of the gem's barbed prongs would cancel out another's power for at least an hour or so. Grand for shaking hands or a close encounter. But something long term, yet not permanent? He had it; for the right price.

Lou took another hit, unchaining the watch from his jacket as he set it on the table. He left the trinket open before him as time slowly ticked forward. She had three minutes to get here. For a busy man like Lou, being on time was considered late. The seconds seemed to pass by on their own accord, carefree of Lou's busy schedule. He perked his head up as the black veil by the door shifted.

The hands on the watch struck midnight as a blonde woman moved through the soundproof veil of the back room. Tardy. He gazed up at the guard before him, pausing in his movements. Maybe this one time he ought to make an exception.

A tall, strong-looking beauty stood before him. Her platinum blonde hair was tied back behind her head in loose, intricate braids, besides a few curls that lingered near the front of her face. Her blue eyes held a soft delicacy that deeply contrasted the rest of her harsh demeanor. Not to mention, a woman in uniform. Aye. He had a type.

"Have a seat, love. You're late." Lou let the words roll off his tongue, extending his arm to indicate the spot beside him. He leaned forward on his elbows, swiping up the watch and tucking it back away into his coat. The Leprechaun's eyes stared at the blue of her gaze, slowly perusing his way downward. She had a nice curve to her hips, especially in that tight-fitting black leather armor.

He paused at the seal of the Winter King on her shoulder. Was this angel about to drag him into hell? Did they know about the prince? Mara was many things, but she wouldn't rat him out. Lou folded his hands together, waiting for the woman to speak before making any assumptions. If anything went down, at least he paid Frank to be here.

The guard's eyes flitted between him and the half-orc at his side. "I'll stand, thank you." She gave him a respectful nod of her head.

"Suit yourself," Lou laughed, rubbing a finger under his nose. A small smirk slid across his expression. "Something tells me you're not at home here, lass."

"I go where duty leads me," she replied.

"How noble. Well, my fine lady, let's start off with introductions. I'm Lou." The Leprechaun leaned across the table, holding out his hand.

The woman's nose twitched as she eyed up his greeting. She postponed the moment, slowly leaning forward to return the gesture. "Kaia."

The guard moved to shake his hand, but he pulled her in unexpectedly. Lou pressed his lips to the back of her glove, wondering how soft her skin felt underneath. "A leather finger tab on your dominant hand, I presume. We have an archer in our presence, Frank." He winked at her and Kaia pulled her hand away, glaring at him before schooling her expression to its neutral state.

"Well, Lady Kaia, it's my pleasure to make your acquaintance," he crooned, the playfulness of his tone giving the guard pause. "And how can I be of assistance?"

"I'm in search of an artifact." The woman was strictly business in her words and tenor. "The bartend at the front spoke highly of your knowledge on the subject."

"Aye, it's true. I know a great deal about many artifacts. Of what variety do you seek?"

"One to cancel out a fae's powers. Not a permanent change, but something longer term," Kaia replied.

Lou let out a low whistle, sitting back against the cushions. He crossed his arms as he pretended to think. "Do you hear that, Frank? A rare item Lady Kaia searches for, indeed . . ."

"Does it exist?" Kaia prompted after a few moments of silence.

Lou nodded. "It does."

"Is it within your skill to acquire it?"

"Already have it, love."

Kaia paused, lips pressing together in a thin line. "Can I see it?"

The leprechaun shook his head, a soft melodic chuckle filling the room as he clasped his hands together. What a riot this beauty was. She really was out of her element, wasn't she? Hopefully not the king's sole negotiator. Then again, it wouldn't be a bad thing for him if she was. She seemed focused on the item, and not actually getting any information out of him.

This could work to his advantage. They didn't know of his connection to the Wicked Prince's abduction. What was the harm in fulfilling a small request, keeping the kingdom off his back, and wiggling himself into a better standing?

"No, my dear. You see, it's impossible for me to carry all my wares on me at once. For security reasons, of course. I can obtain the item if that be your request. I do happen to have a necklace that can perform the requirements that you seek, but . . ."

"It comes with a price," Kaia finished.

The Leprechaun laughed, tilting his head back. "Aye, what a smart lass. That it does."

"What is your wish?"

"What is my wish?" He turned to his bodyguard. "I like this girl, I do." He faced back in her direction with a grin. "I wish of one thing. Simple, really. I want nothing more than to return to my homeland." He put a hand over his heart. "I can't express how much I miss my family. Me poor mum, she must be worried sick."

Kaia frowned at him. "I'm afraid I don't understand. All you want . . .is to go to Faerie? Why don't you just find a portal?"

"Well, a portal alone isn't helpful to my circumstance. You see, I've been exiled. Banished. Kicked out."

Kaia's pupils widened and he looked on as she failed to hide her surprise. It was not often that one was barred from entering the realm, and yet here he sat, requesting to get back in.

"Exiled from Faerie?"

"As I said. And I will give you the necklace you seek in exchange for returning home."

The king's guard grew quiet, taking in his words. "How do you know if I can grant that wish? I lack the level of authority to—"

Lou scoffed. "Lady Kaia, allow me to cut through your bullshit. That insignia on your shoulder. Aye, that one. I know what it is. It is clear you're a woman of great power and talent to be at the side of the king. I reckon' you're smart enough to find a way to make this happen. If not, well . . . you are quite beautiful and that's all some lasses need to get by." Lou stood up from the table, grabbing his pipe. He pushed his thumb into the bowl to pack the lavender down before shoving it into one of his inside pockets. "Shall we get going, Frank?"

"Yes, sir," the bodyguard nodded.

"Wait. Fine. Yes, I'll . . . I'll look into it," Kaia said through gritted teeth.

"Just look into it?" Lou put on his best frown, scratching the bottom of his chin. "Oh, I don't know if it's worth my time if you're only going to consider it."

"I'll make it happen," Kaia corrected, narrowing her eyes at him.

"That's a lass." Lou smiled, walking over to stand in front of her. "I knew I could count on a woman as reliable as yourself. Meet me here . . ." He paused, fishing out his watch once more. "Midday tomorrow. Complete my request and the necklace is all yours. Oh, and don't be late this time. It's just bad manners." He gave Kaia a wink, ducking through the black veil that covered the door. The half-orc followed closely at his side like a trained dog. A devious smirk crossed him as he headed down the hallway, fighting the need to click his heels. He couldn't celebrate just yet.

"Lou," the angel called out his name from behind, the Leprechaun returning to a look of innocence but not yet facing Kaia. He waited, knowing she would speak first.

She walked a few steps closer then asked, "Before I do this, I need to know. Why were you exiled from Faerie?"

Lou chuckled, rubbing at the corner of his mouth as he slowly turned to face Kaia. "Ah, love, that is the question, isn't it? It's because I stole the Amulet of Morgan Le Fae."

MARA

The world shifted underneath her, conscious or unaware . . . did it matter? Mara's mind floated, eyes, mouth, and wrists burning. To lay in bed all day, the comfort of the world teasing her. She fought against the needs of her body, not quite coming to terms with the situation of her captivity. She allowed her eyes to droop shut. She craved release, fighting against being stuck in this hellscape. While sleep would allow for freedom of her mind, Mara was terrified of what might happen the moment she was unaware and compliant.

Still, if she were to continue to fight against the Winter King, she would need all the energy that she could muster. Mara listened to the incessant scribbling of the man's quill scratching the parchment from across the room. Vareck had settled long ago at his desk, allowing the fae some reprieve from his advances. If he was still that far, perhaps she could let her eyes close once more. If only for a moment . . .

Her body drifted, pulling against the edges of sleep. To rest now for the later fight was the greatest reprieve a warrior could ask for. With the emptiness of her mind, she tucked away any worries that appeared in anxious whispers. What would Sadie do when she found her apartment empty along with the hideout? Would the shop close without her tending to it? Another month of missed payments passed her by. While these problems were real, it kept her mind safe from the current situation, letting herself be lulled to sleep.

A loud pair of footsteps traveled down the hallway outside, Mara's eyes snapping open. Alert, she sat up, facing the door a moment before a knock echoed through the room and she heard Kaia's announce herself. Vareck glanced between the her shifting and the arrival of the unexpected guest, standing up from his desk. "You may enter," he called out.

The large doors swung open as Vareck rubbed at the bags under his eyes, watching as Kaia stood entered the room and went to Vareck's desk with an all too familiar man at her side. He had a scruffy ginger beard that matched his hair and his eyes were as green as the money he surely wished to acquire.

Shock crossed Mara as she watched the pair, eyes darting between old acquaintances and new. If only she could scream out, say something, or perhaps even strangle the leprechaun before her eyes. She cursed him through her gag, the muffled sound drawing their attention. Lou looked at her, surprise coloring his usually smug face.

"This is the one?" Vareck asked, groaning, bringing the attention back to him.

Kaia placed a hand over her chest, bowing deeply. "Yes, Your Grace," Lou followed suit in her gesture, bowing before the king, ignoring Mara.

"Of course, it would be," he muttered. Raising his voice again, he said, "I don't trust this—nor do I trust leprechauns. But if you have what I need, I'll allow you to stay."

"Aye, of course, Your Majesty. If you don't trust me, trust in the fine advice of Lady Kaia. I am happy to once again serve my king." He bowed once more, Mara rolling her eyes. *Lady Kaia. Mmpfh.* It wasn't unlike Lou to try to gain what he wanted through thick layers of flattery. But, why was he here?

"Very well," the king mused, turning to look at Kaia for further clarification.

"Lou was the contact I met at the Witching Hour," Kaia began, holding her hands together in front of her body. Mara squinted over at Lou, mostly in a glare as she watched him intensely focus on Kaia as she talked. "With Lou's assistance, I believe we've found an answer to your request, King Vareck."

"Well, what is it?" The king folded his arms, incredulous as he waited for some sort of parlor trick to appear from the leprechaun. Lou shifted through a bag at his side, looking in a similar material to that of his trench coat. He fished around for a few moments, pulling out a magnificent piece of jewelry. The necklace shined as light hit the surface, the beautiful crystal at the center of the medallion glistening.

Mara felt her heart jump, panic coursing through her. That necklace . . . that damned necklace. Lou wouldn't, he couldn't. She curled up, placing her foot against the binds of her hands and clawing to break free of what held her. If she lost her magic, her one opportunity to escape—damn it, Lou. She stole that necklace for him, and this was Lou's way to repay her? Dead. He was dead. Beyond dead. She would kill him, find a way to resurrect him, and then murder him again!

"Cursed artifacts are my specialty. They're easily acquired when nobody wants them, but incredibly useful for reasons we don't expect." Lou placed a hand under the gem, showing off the necklace between the King and Kaia. "This necklace drains the power of the one that wears it, stores it in the gem. Once the necklace is removed, that power returns. However, the wearer itself cannot take it off. Impressive, aye?" Lou asked, glancing over at the guard for a long moment before shifting his gaze to the king.

"If it does as you say, then yes. Yes, it is," Vareck said, extending his hand. Lou placed the medallion part of the necklace into his palm, the king admiring its beauty. "Only one way to find out if your words are true, and for your sake, you'd better hope they are." The king moved from the pair walking over to the side of the bed. Mara watched with wide eyes, scrambling to move away from him as they all turned to look at her. "Stay still," he commanded.

She felt her body turn to stone; limbs heavy at the pull of his magic. She gritted her teeth around the gag as Vareck placed the necklace over her head. Mara's shoulders drooped, feeling the unfamiliar sensation of power leaving her body slowly, draining away until it was gone entirely. The woman shut her eyes tight, seething as the king moved to untie her hands.

"I'm going to untie you. Do not attack anyone," Vareck commanded.

Mara's hands clenched into fists as he removed the gag, the woman standing up and pushing past the king immediately. She stormed over to Lou, fire roaring in her gaze. "When," she hissed, voice loud and clear even with edge of hoarseness from days of slight dehydration. "When. Not if. *When* I get out of here, you're dead." She grabbed the corner of his dark green vest, willing her body to knock Lou across the face.

Her hand couldn't move, numb to the action that went against Vareck's wishes. Trapped. She had never felt so trapped. The woman snarled, letting go of Lou and turning away towards the window as her rage boiled.

"Aw, Mara. Don't be that way," Lou said and

winked at her. "You know I've always been fond of you. But it's only business, love."

Vareck's head snapped towards the leprechaun at the use of the word, his entire body tensing, a growl emitting from the back of his throat.

Kaia stepped forward and grabbed Lou by the shoulder, gently guiding him back towards the door. "Lovely job, Lou. Why don't we get out of here? I suggest that the king might need a moment, yes?" Her hand grasped towards the door, missing the knob the first time before successfully getting it open.

Lou seemed to chipper up at the suggestion, gladly taking the opportunity to head out. "Of course," he hummed. "Aye, let's find a place where the two of us can chat and I can buy you a drink. See where the day takes us." Kaia let go of his shoulder, glancing between Lou and Vareck from the side of her vision as the two headed out the door.

One minute passed, and then another. Mara supported herself against the lone bookcase on the side wall near the window. It was just the two of them now, along with an old magic cat—or whatever he was—who softly snored as he lay upside-down on the corner of the bed. The room could go up in flames and the familiar would still be content to nap.

Mara shut her eyes tightly. With this freedom of movement and speech came the captivity of her spirit. She needed to get away from the king. The huntress desperately craved a change of scenery and just the simple comfort of space alone from anyone else.

"I'm taking a bath," Mara grunted, marching into the bathroom chamber like a child, the door slamming behind her. It felt good. It felt so good to get the unused energy out. She wanted to push things further, punch, kick, scream. She locked the door, hands gripping onto the side of the sink. Her eyes wandered to gaze at her reflection, not even recognizing the figure before her. Worn, sleep-deprived, her hair was tangled into knots. The creature who gazed back from the reflection was not Mara. She was a prisoner.

She heard Vareck move to the door, but he didn't try to come in. He called from the other room, finally giving her some respectful space. "Mara, do not hurt yourself or make any attempts to escape," he commanded gently.

Mara sighed as his magic coursed through her, turning the knob of the tub. Hot water poured into the basin as her hands move across different untouched soaps. Were these for her? The king had never smelled of such floral scents. Her mood dipped again, pissed that she was getting intimate enough with the king to recognize what he smelled like.

He may have a strong persuasion, and she may not have her powers, but she didn't need them to get out. She stripped herself of the old clothes, skin more than grateful to breath. One foot slipped into the water, then the other, blindly grabbing one of the bars of soap.

"Mara?" Vareck asked hesitantly by the door. "Can I bring you . . . something?"

"Just . . . leave me alone." She sunk into the water, letting her hair float on the surface. Letting out a deep sigh, she slipped into the depths, the sounds muffling around her as she closed her eyes.

VARECK

Vareck understood that it took a woman a while to get ready. However, this long was ridiculous. Hours had passed since Mara had locked herself away in the bathroom. He worked at his desk, trying to busy his mind. Still he knew she was avoiding him at this point. If it weren't for the fact that he could feel his mate bond, he would have stormed into the room.

A long sigh pulled itself from the king's lips. She sounded so sad when she had asked for space. This much he needed to grant to her if he wanted Mara to feel comfortable here. Still . . . Vareck grunted, cursing under his breath as a quill broke in his hand. He pushed himself away from the desk, running a hand through his long hair.

At least he didn't have to deal with the constantly draining magic any longer. However, with the strain and exhaustion waning, his primal need to claim her was beginning to gnaw at his core. It had been blessedly less noticeable when he was using every bit of himself to control her. His fingertips drummed against the arm of the chair, trying to find something to distract himself. The more he focused his efforts on the paperwork in front of him, the more his mind wandered to the woman soaking in the tub.

Vareck was determined to learn more discipline within himself. Move his thoughts away from her body when he first needed to win over her heart. Deep down, the ways he wished to ravage his mate concerned him. He didn't want to hurt Mara. He wanted her to want him. He wanted to learn how to love her.

A thick fluffy body hopped up to the corner of the desk. Corvo nudged an open ink well towards the side with his paw. The bottle precariously stopped at the edge. Vareck quirked a brow, swiping away the ink and placing it across from the cat at a safe distance, making sure to cork the bottle.

"Must you?" he huffed, reaching over to scratch his familiar behind the ears.

"I must. You've got that thousand-yard stare, V. I know a million things are going on in that mind of yours. I mean, I can hear it all. Gotta say, though. I'm getting a little sick of how much you think about wanting to—"

The king hushed the cat, rubbing underneath Corvo's chin. "How in the world was I so blessed to come across you as my demon guardian?" Vareck mused dryly.

Corvo chuckled, letting out a rumbling purr. "Hey. Whatever I can do to cheer you up, I try it."

"Please don't."

"Look, why don't try to you get her something? Woman like things, right?"

"Extensive knowledge on the subject now? I know you sneak off at night, but I had no idea it was for courting the rogue cats in the castle."

"I'm a master in observation and I decided long ago that the best advice was given based on inexperience. So, are you going to get her something, or what?"

Vareck contemplated his familiar's words, sitting back in his chair as he rubbed at the scruff of his beard. What would Mara even like? "I got her a necklace."

Corvo settled down, tucking his paws underneath himself in a condensed loaf. The cat did not look pleased, waiting for the king to suggest another item.

"What?" Vareck mused.

"V, you really are dense. That doesn't count, and you know it," Corvo meowed. Vareck glanced to the side, nodding as he breathed out gruffly.

"Yeah, I know." To even consider a gift to Mara with how much hatred she currently held for him ... where would he even begin? Flowers? Chocolates? This wasn't a normal form of courting by any means. His mother had told him from quite an early age that it would be easy once he found his mate. Vareck had expected some sort of playful resilience, but never in his mind had he expected the woman of his dreams to passionately hate him.

The bathroom door creaked open, interrupting his thoughts. Mara stepped into the room; a white camisole blouse draped across her shoulders. The piece didn't quite reach her bellybutton, a section of her pale stomach exposed before the rest of her body was shrouded by a long, sheer but gauzy skirt. The material hid her slender legs as it gracefully met the floor. Vareck was speechless.

Amazing how a bath and a set of fresh clothes could make her every bit as beautiful and befitting as the title of the future queen. He had decided that, from this point forward, she could take however long she wanted to get ready if this was the result. Maybe this was all the cravings of not seeing her form for so long, but Vareck didn't care. He just wanted to keep admiring her beauty. The moment his eyes caught her expression, the fantasy before him disappeared. She looked anything but pleased.

"Hello," he began, the words a bit stiff and hesitant. "I hope you, uh, enjoyed your bath." He cleared his throat. "Can we talk?"

"I need new clothes," she demanded, arms wrapping around herself. "It's freezing. Everywhere. And this"—her arms moved down her waist, Vareck's gaze involuntarily following—"is ridiculous."

The king blinked, surprised at how Mara went

from glaring and unresponsive to making demands. "If that is what you wish, then yes. I will send for new clothes after you agree to talk. Does that sound like a fair compromise?"

Mara huffed, returning her arms to wrap around herself, giving Vareck a few nods with her head.

"Let's sit by the fire," the king insisted, holding his arm out in a polite gesture. She waited, staring blankly for a moment before obliging his suggestion. Mara moved to position herself at the foot of the bed, the nearest spot to the fireplace. Vareck walked to a chest near the bookshelf, lifting the hatches as he moves down on one knee. Shuffling through the box's contents, he soon found what he was looking for.

He placed a thick blanket on Mara's lap, the woman looking at it carefully before curling her fingers into the intricate crochet stitching. "Thank you." He heard the words, but they caught him off guard, her expression of gratitude was highly unexpected.

"Of course." Vareck watched as she unfolded the dark blue blanket, unfurling it fully before wrapping it around her shoulders. She glanced at him briefly before turning back to the flames. The king had noticed on recent observations that while he seemed to stare at the world outside, his mate would sit on the bed, spending her time watching the flames crackle. How different were their worlds, their perspectives?

Still, even while Mara seemed encapsulated by the dancing flames and crackling roar, there was something missing from her features. Vareck would say that it was her smile, but it was more than that. For even if she managed a tilt of her lips, he doubted it would reach her eyes. She was suffering, and he knew he was the cause of it.

He hated it, truly. Hated himself more for forcing things to be this way. But she would run, and she wouldn't listen. If she would just take the time to hear him out and if he could learn how to control these unholy urges just long enough . . . Vareck's hands curled into fists, flinching as his nails dug into his palms.

Mara was the first to speak, breaking the silence stretching between them. "So, you wanted to talk?"

"I want to get to know you," Vareck replied, pulling over his desk chair to sit beside her while granting her a respectful space.

"That's what I don't get. Why? I doubt that you'd care about my favorite color or"—she paused as if she was searching for the right words—"where I grew up, or what my favorite Beatles song is."

"A beetle? Like a . . . like a bug?" Vareck asked, brows furrowing as he sat forward, clasping his hands together. He was trying to keep his posture relaxed; trying to be as open as possible.

Mara let out a huff of a laugh, shaking her head as she brought the blanket closer to herself. "No. They're a—never mind, forget it."

"Mara, you mistake me. I want to know these things. You are my mate."

She snorted derisively. "Am I your mate? Or am I your pet? You've kidnapped me, held me against my will, and now you even have a collar to keep me." Her words dripped in venom, fingers moving up to the lock of the necklace, her fingernails extending to a sharper form. *That's not a high fae trait . . . interesting.* He wondered if she realized she was doing it. If she realized the strength of whatever this magic was. It was responding to her . . . not the other way around.

Vareck bit his bottom lip, turning his eyes away as she fiddled with the artifact. "I don't wish for things to be this way. You left me no choice."

"Why should I have stopped trying to run from you when this is the outcome?" Mara bit back, throwing her arms down from her neck as an anger began to boil beneath the surface. "I'm trapped, cut from my magic, removed from my family, and have no contacts in this world besides you and that damned cat."

"Hey." Corvo picked his head up from one of the pillows near the other side of the bed. It seemed that he had moved from the desk.

Vareck sighed, taking the lashing with grace. "You are my mate. Once you see this, and I come to trust you and you come to trust me, we can move past it all." Not even he sounded sure of his words.

"You keep saying that, but you can't blame me for

not believing you. I have stood true to the fact that mate bonds don't exist. It's just dumb folktale nonsense to get you to believe in love. For how important it's supposed to be, wouldn't I have felt something?"

"It . . ." He hesitated, chewing on his words. "There is a reason for it, I swear."

"Tell me, then," Mara replied, turning away from the fire to face him. "If you want me to believe you—to trust you—tell me."

"It's a long story."

"I seem to have an abundance of time," Mara quipped.

Vareck let out a laugh. "I suppose I deserve that." He licked his lips, moving through the timeline of the stories in his head. With something plaguing the lands for hundreds of years, where did he start?

"At the beginning. You start at the beginning," Corvo chided.

"Yes, *thank you,* Corvo. Shouldn't you be napping?" Vareck said. Mara looked between him and the cat, confused.

Vareck took a deep breath and began. "Long ago, the people of Faerie and the high fae within the realm were cursed—"

"You can't be serious. Once upon a time? What, is there a magical sword and a prophecy to match?"

"This is what I meant about not listening. And yes. There is a prophecy, or really, I should say that there was a prophecy. It's already happened. Now, do you want to hear about the mate bond, or no?"

Mara puffed out her cheeks and nodded grimly, glancing to the side. Vareck took her silence as permission to continue.

"Long ago, the people of Faerie and the high fae within the realm were cursed," he started again, pausing to see if Mara would interrupt him. The woman rolled her eyes, gesturing with her hand for him to continue. "The king that ruled was wicked, evil, and tormenting in his ways. He enjoyed his life and the power he held over the fae in the realm. One day, a banshee foretold that a harpy would be the death of him. So, in order to change his fate, he put out an order to slay all the harpies in the land. Every last one . . ."

Mara frowned; brows furrowed as the story clearly began to pique her interest. "He ordered a mass killing? It sounds like this is going to be a self-fulfilling prophecy."

The corner of Vareck's lip turned upward, the faintest smile playing at his expression. "Aren't all prophecies self-fulfilling, really?"

"I suppose so," Mara said, glancing down to look at her hands. "What happened with the harpies? Did they all die?"

Vareck chuckled, mentally backtracking to his place in the story. "Glad to see I have caught your interest. They did, yes. A harpy has a unique gift; they are given one curse in their lifetime. They call it true upon their death, and through their magic, their will makes it reality. After the Corrupt King called for this decree, a group of harpies banded together. They cursed the high fae and all of Faerie to grow barren and die, the mate bond with it. So since then, the land has been tormented through an eternal winter."

"An eternal winter? But why? Why curse all the high fae? Why not just the king? They would punish everyone for the actions of their ruler?"

"They believed the high fae needed to be punished for being passive bystanders. They did nothing while their king committed genocide."

"But it wasn't their fault. The king controls all of the armed forces, and most of the people are just simple farmers, or whatever else it is that people do here."

"No, you are correct. It wasn't' fair. That's why one harpy, a young woman, decided to redirect the curse. She knew in her heart it was not enough to cancel it effects. However, she could add a loophole, so to speak. Add a way that the curse could be broken."

Vareck rubbed his thumb against the back of his hand, gaze staring off as he repeated the words burned into his memory. *"Summer comes on shadow wings. A half fae will be born with hair like the dawn and eyes of the forest in winter's depths. She will be the mate to the king, and upon their union the curse will begin to unravel."*

Mara stared at him skeptically, leaving him to continue speaking.

"I know this might all be hard to believe, but try. The land will continue to wither and die without you. You—our bond—they're the key to unraveling the curse."

"I'm not dumb," Mara retorted. "You really expect me to believe that you only want to fuck me to save your people?" He flinched at the harshness of her words. "You're the Winter King. There's as much cold and unfeeling in this land as there is in your name."

Vareck sat up, posture straightening at her words as he forced himself to bite his tongue. "I am not the evil you or this realm believe me to be. I have done nothing to hurt you. I have done everything to try and keep you comfortable; to keep you safe. Your scent is intoxicating, and you have no idea the restraint it takes when every fiber of my being wants to claim you. I want you and it has nothing to do with my people. I lost faith in them until I felt your pull the night of the ball. I want you to have a choice, but I also cannot help but wanting you to choose me. To choose our bond." He shook his head, not sure how to get the words through to Mara now that he had the chance.

"The bond I can't feel," Mara remarked, voice not as strong.

Vareck nodded. "The bond you cannot feel."

The woman faced back to the flames of the hearth, staring at the embers of the glowing coals. Her mind seemed to wander off before him, deep in thought. He let her stew for a few minutes, gently prompting a question. "What are you thinking about?"

"I guess I've always known about the endless winter. That there was a curse on Faerie even if I didn't know its origins." She shifted on the bed, bringing her legs up to rest on the frame instead of on the floor. "My family used to live here, but they said they had to leave. Migrated to the human realm because the food was so scarce that they couldn't survive. My mother always said that the small fae everywhere were suffering and just the thought of being able to end that is . . . well, it's something else." She let out a soft sigh. "I think it sucks. If I'm this woman you envision in this counter-curse, or whatever it's called, then why don't I feel anything? You are holding me captive. You've stripped me of my powers, I'm relying on the word of a deranged fae king, I was betrayed by someone I trusted—I'm still going to kill him, that fucking backstabbing weasel—I'm probably worrying my sister sick, and really, why the hell is it all on me getting married to save Faerie? All I wanted was to pay my rent and get a damn puppy. Was that too much to ask?" Mara's chest heaved as she searched for a breath, Vareck watching her with wide eyes.

She gulped in air, trying to steady herself from the rant. "It's super not cool to use persuasion on me when I can't use it on you."

"I have no way of understanding you or knowing what is really going on in your mind unless you tell me," Vareck replied simply, not seeing anything wrong with his tactics.

"Yeah, but you don't have the right to make the demand of me every time you want something. I'm trying to process all of this. Just ask first. It's not that hard."

"Fair enough." Vareck sat back slowly. Never had he been so enthralled to know everything about someone. He hadn't meant to push her away as he tried to move forward with their connection. Vareck lived for these little tidbits of her life.

Mara sighed; frown settling deep upon her face. "I'm going to bed. Keep up your end of the deal about the new clothes. If they're not here when I get up, you can't be mad at me for turning the fur blankets into dresses."

He nodded slowly, watching as she moved into bed. Mara placed the blanket over her usual spot, soon curling up into the sheets. Vareck sat and watched her for a few moments longer. His arms crossed as he watched her turn away from him. "Sweet dreams, Mara."

She didn't reply, a handful of minutes passing by. Her shoulders moved with her body with each graceful breath. How content she seemed in the moment, free of any thoughts about the future as she dreamed.

It's was only when he was sure she was deep in slumber that Vareck made his way to the opposite side of the bed. He shooed the cat aside, Corvo grumbling at being disturbed. The cat jumped down, trotting over to the reading nook where he wouldn't have to share space.

Vareck unbuttoned his shirt, pulling it off and tossing it to the side of the bed as he crawled under the sheets beside her. Just to be near her and her scent. Know that he would keep her safe, even from herself. With the warmth of the blankets and the chill of the crisp air, it wasn't long before the combination helped to fade his mind into the darkness. For living in this castle for the last six hundred years, this was perhaps the first time he had ever felt at home.

MARA

❋

Mara clawed at the sheets, back arching against the bed. Her head rolled to the side as warmth fueled through her body. The call of sleep still pulled at Mara's being, curling in closer when a pair of strong arms wrapped around her. It felt so good to be encapsulated, ensnared by comfort. A soft sigh left her lips as another body pressed against her own.

She wanted to stay in this dream. It felt too good to leave it. The way teeth lightly grazed down her neck and an erection pressed up against her ass. She inhaled sharply moving her hips back against the dream in reward for the delectable sensation. The warmth shifted, the dream trailing his arms down lower on her body. Strong hands passed over her bare stomach, devouring every part of her exposed skin, sending shocks of electricity through her system.

Mara bit down on her bottom lip as the palms

diverged. One hand lingered up towards her breast, trailing their fingertips against her. A chill ran through her body at the anticipation. The dream ran its thumb against her nipple, teasing as a soft moan pulled itself from her throat. Encouraged by this reaction, the hand continued. The strokes turned to kneading, demanding as it explored how she would react.

Each gasp, each roll of her hips against the dream's hard length encouraged the confidence to take, and take, and take. The other hand slipped between her legs, sliding under her skirt against the soft silk of her panties. A loud groan rumbled out from the back of her throat, almost primal in the way she whimpered. The pleasant feeling built up from deep within her core, fingers slipping inside her—filling her—desire burning with each stroke.

To be touched this way. To feel skin on skin . . . it had been so long . . . it felt so good.

She rocked her hips, greedily grinding forward against the hand between her legs and pressing into the cock behind her. Mara tilted her head back, senses overloaded as she awoke with a sharp gasp; her muscles spasmed, a flood of heat burning through her as she found her release and she tried to catch her breath.

She slowly blinked away the haze, the daze of the orgasm still clouding her senses like a fog. While some parts of her sleep vanished, other parts of the fantasy remained in her dreamy state. The strong arms around her held true, the warmth at her back keeping her safe, the feeling of—

Her eyes widened as she came to realize he was there. She had been grinding her body against Vareck. Was it Vareck? Please be Vareck...wait. No . . .

Mara's spine stiffened as an approving growl rumbled in her ear. "Holy shit," she hissed, quickly throwing the covers down and scrambling to move away from the dreamscape intruder. Mara managed to stand, adjusting her skirt before grabbing a pillow to shield her body. She bared her teeth at the king, fangs extending, and growling out, "What the hell do you think you're doing?"

"What?" Vareck sat up, a lazy smirk across his lips. The covers barely managed to hide his abs as he stretched his arms up over his head. The king yawned, looking quite pleased with himself.

"Y-you can't just do that to someone when they're asleep!" Mara hissed, hugging the pillow tighter to her body, trying to ignore the curves of his chest.

"I don't have the slightest idea what you mean. I was sleeping soundly when a warm, beautiful body started to grind up against me. I was simply reacting to its requests."

"You . . ." she stammered, glaring at him and pointing her finger. "I . . . you . . . I was sleeping!"

"And at first, so was I." The king shrugged, not bothering to hide the confident, crooked smile that lingered across his lips.

She didn't want to admit how turned on her body remained at the image of him sprawled across the bed, or how good his fingers felt inside her. Still, she was pissed. Mara glared him down as she quietly fumed, a tense moment passing in the silence between them. Curse her body for reacting in such a way. Was there some truth to all this mate bond nonsense? For her body to . . . do whatever it just did. It was mortifying.

The worst part was how much she enjoyed it. No, the worst part was that she wanted more. Maybe if next time she could stay asleep and then die of embarrassment before she woke up, then everything would be okay.

No, there wouldn't be a next time. This was a one-time thing with an evil king that—well, a slightly evil king. He's okay. *Alright, besides the fact that he's pushed my boundaries, he hasn't done anything to abuse or hurt me.*

And with the story of the cursed realm yesterday, was it all true that their union would make everything right? She was getting a headache, and everything was so scrambled in her mind. She couldn't make one thought coherently connect to the next.

Mara brought the pillow back, pelting it across the bed at the king. It didn't go against any of his wishes, she would hardly consider it an attack. Vareck let out a short huff at her antics, but before he could react further there was a knock at the door. They exchanged a glance before Vareck pulled himself from the bed, giving himself time to adjust his erection before saying, "Enter."

The king swiped his shirt from the day before off the ground as the grand oak doors opened. Mara stepped back defensively, always on high alert when someone entered the room. It wasn't that she was scared, but the events of the morning had the slightest dusting of pink running across her cheeks.

A tall, muscular high fae dressed in the armor of the King entered. His hair was as black as the ravens that perched on the dead trees in the royal gardens. Behind the thick armor, Mara could see slivers of ink gracing his skin. Tattoos wrapped up from his collarbone, curling up to behind his ears. Even as he stepped, his feet didn't seem to make a sound. The man was as silent as the shadows that lingered over him.

Vareck buttoned up his shirt, greeting the man as the guard bowed before him. "Dorian. Unusual to see you on this side of the castle. What brings you?"

The man placed his left hand over his chest, curling his fist as he bowed. "Your Grace." He paused to glance between her and Vareck. Dorian cleared his throat, the makings of a smile twitching at the corners of his eyes. "I hope I'm not interrupting anything."

"Nothing at all," Vareck mused, crossing his arms. "We were just getting up. Where is Kaia this morning?"

"Not impressed by my presence? You can't have all the ladies at your whim, Your Majesty. I believe this morning she's still being trailed by her annoying admirer." The guard's lips curved into a crooked smirk, clasping his hands behind his back as he widened his stance, the width of his broad shoulders seeming to swallow the space between the doors.

"He's still here?" Mara moved forward to grab the frame of the bed, fingers curling around the pole. "That leprechaun has a death wish. Hope you hid your silver."

Dorian seemed amused by her spark and he barked out a laugh.

Vareck looked at Dorian in surprise. "I wasn't aware that Kaia had an admirer. That should be interesting to see. But I doubt you came to tell me about Kaia's love life. So, what news do you have to ruin my morning?"

Turning serious, he said, "It is a concern of the realm, Your Majesty. There have been no new leads on Prince Sebastian's disappearance."

"Yes? And?" Vareck asked, shoulders shrugging as his arms crossed in front of him.

Mara walked forward, settling herself next to the two men in order to physically insert herself into the conversation. "I'm curious. Why don't you care that your own nephew is missing?"

Vareck's expression soured, lips pressing together. His body stiffened and his eyes narrowed. She could feel the tension rolling off him in waves.

She tilted her head slightly, wondering why he

went quiet and why the sudden change. A memory flashed in her mind. When Vareck had found her kissing Sebastian, his anger was enough to make the hair on the back of her neck stand straight up. Mara rubbed at her shoulder, as if the memory alone was enough to trigger the fear in that moment. But something now mingled with it, muddying her thoughts. It was almost as if she could *feel* the emotion coursing through him . . . was it jealousy?

Dorian filled in the silence. "Sebastian is the heir. Lady Elena wants to know what is being done to find him. She is beside herself and I have no answers."

Vareck sighed, moving a hand up to pinch at the bridge of his nose. "Alright, let's find out," Vareck said, turning to her. "Mara, where is Sebastian?"

She shrugged, putting her hands out. "I've been here the last week. How would I know? I was in my apartment minding my own business when *someone* bound and gagged me, and not in a fun way."

Vareck's eyes flashed, a look so heated she felt an aching throb between her legs. He lifted her chin towards him, his fangs extending as he growled, "Do not tempt me, Huntress. My desire to claim you is strong, and your suggestive comments don't make it easier to deny myself." She stood her ground and returned the stare, but she felt what moxie she had waver as he towered over her. "One more chance. Let's do this right. Tell me what you know. I would rather give you the opportunity to speak freely, as it is your wish," he said as he released her chin and took a step back.

Turned on. Confused. Annoyed. She took a deep breath. "I'm being honest with you. I don't know where Sebastian is. Why don't you go ahead and ask the asshole magical arms dealer you let wander amongst you? Lou's the one that paid me to snatch him, after all."

Both the king and the guard stood shocked by her proclamation. "What? Why didn't you say something?"

"Because you had me gagged! And honestly, yesterday I was really mad at you. And before you say anything, yes, I'm still mad at you."

"I—never mind. Dorian, question him."

"I can do that, but I bet Kaia would have a better chance of getting him to talk, seeing as how he's trying to get in her—"

"Dorian," Vareck snapped. "I don't care who asks the leprechaun, just get it done. Now."

Dorian straightened immediately, bowing before the king. "Yes, Your Majesty."

VARECK

The guard swiftly moved out the door before Vareck had a chance to say another word. What in the world had Kaia gotten herself into by bringing that leprechaun here?

"Thank you."

Once again, the words from her lips surprised him. He turned towards her, anger melting away. What did she have to be thankful for? She'd just said she was angry with him. Mara seemed to know he was at a loss, continuing her words. "For listening. You didn't use your persuasion on me when you easily could have commanded an answer right away. I appreciate that."

He nodded his response and carefully weighed the situation as he moved over to his closet. He shuffled through the wardrobe, pausing at the remembrance that he needed to send for new clothes for his mate.

Lest she turn the blankets into her threatened fur dresses. Oh, what a sight that would be.

Vareck picked out a warm sweater knit by the finest pixie weavers in the land. The king headed back over, handing her the item of clothing.

"Wear this for now. I will send for new clothes as soon as I speak with the staff. I want you to be comfortable here. Having you make your own choices and be your own person falls in that category. I am struggling, but I never want to force you into anything."

"Don't push your sentiments too hard. I'm still your kidnapped prisoner with a collar." Mara turned, hesitant before pulling the deep green piece over her head.

It was far too big for her, the woman practically drowned in it as it landed around her thighs. Her arms disappeared in the sleeves before beginning to roll them up. Vareck didn't mind seeing her in his clothes. Was it wrong to like how his scent was lingering over her?

"I've already said that this is not the way I intended things to be. As my mate, I want you to learn to trust me and my actions."

"I would trust you more if I had my freedom."

"And I you, if there was not the threat of you jumping out of the windows," Vareck countered, a small smirk curling up his lips. Mara didn't seem to have a retort at first, rolling her eyes as she sat on the cushions by the reading nook. Corvo was napping there, and Mara dared to extend her fingers to scratch behind his ears.

The cat purred, not bothering to move as he allowed the interaction. Vareck watched from afar, giving the woman her space as she seemed to be mulling something over. Soon enough, she spoke up once more.

"Why don't you care about the well-being of the prince?" Her eyes turned to focus on Vareck's form, changing the conversation entirely. He'd much rather talk for hours about her than about his dreaded nephew.

"Sebastian and I," Vareck began, leaning against the corner of the desk, "we do not see eye to eye. He has different viewpoints on the future of the realm that I simply do not agree with. While they might please the people, it will only hurt Faerie as a whole." Vareck turned to the side, letting out a small huff. "Also, he is a complete asshole."

Mara laughed, curling the rest of her body into the nook. She tilted her head to the side as she gazed upon him.

"What?" He grinned, taking in his new favorite sound.

"Nothing," Mara said, wrapping her arms around her knees. "Weren't you looking for a new shirt?"

Vareck chuckled. "Yes, but I was concerned for the safety of my bedding." Mara rolled her eyes, this time almost playful in nature. She watched him as he pulled himself up to return to the closet. He unbuttoned the old shirt, tossing it into a hamper on the side of the rack.

"No assistants to dress you?" Mara teased.

"Why? Are you volunteering to undress me, Mara?" he asked, turning toward her, a playful smile on his face. He could see the heat return to Mara's cheeks as look at his shirtless body.

Mara forced her gaze away. "Nice try." He laughed, returning to the task at hand as he ducked back into his wardrobe to gather an outfit. A few moments of comfortable silence passed between them as Vareck shifted around hangers.

"Can I ask you something?" he said, returning in a new pair of pants and pulling a shirt over his head.

"You may," Mara answered, looking at him curiously.

"Why is it that you kidnap people for the leprechaun? You don't seem fond of him."

"I'm not. Fond of him, I mean. Not anymore. As far as the jobs go, I'm just trying to pay my bills." Her fingers played with the hem of the sweater, glancing down at the intricate green knit. "I'm not usually dealing with people. Mostly items of importance or artifacts. Like this necklace, for example, which I now regret ever finding." Her tone turned a bit harsh, eyes narrowing at her admission.

She sighed, letting her breath out slowly as though she was attempting to regain control of herself. He waited patiently, trying to give her the space she needed to trust him. To feel comfortable telling him things. "Artifacts are interesting to me," she continued. "These days, people—humans—don't usually appreciate antiques and the quality of pieces that I find, so Lou is easy to sell to. Everything I have ever held in my hands"—Mara paused to pick you a book—"has a history. Has a story of its own. Not only its origins, but who put their heart and soul into making it, and in who it had once belonged to. Can you imagine? If it could speak, what stories would it tell?"

Mara tilted her head, flipping the cover over. Her fingertips gently trailed down the page. "Just thinking about this book makes me wonder so many questions. Who wrote it and why? Where did they write it; was it at a desk by candlelight, or on a blanket in a field? Where did the ink come from? What about the tree that once stood in the forest that someone chopped down to make the pages? I love it all." The woman blinked, pulling herself out of the trance as she shut her mouth and closed the novel.

Vareck stepped forward, desperate for her to continue. He was enthralled by every breath she took. "I agree." He searched his mind, trying to quickly come up with a response that would encourage her to talk further. "History is important and can teach us much about who we can become. Or what mistakes we should learn from. I have always appreciated the allure of a story, even the way that it is skewed from the mouth of the storyteller." Thinking on what else he could say, he added, "I saw your shop while I was in the human realm."

Mara's eyebrows went up in surprise. "You did? How did you know it was mine?"

"Your scent. You must spend a lot of time there. It was the first place I was led to, but I couldn't feel your presence there." It felt like a strange answer, Vareck clearing his throat before trying to change the subject once more. "The store had an incredible number of items for display, and I would be honored to see more of it. The human realm holds many things that we of Faerie have never experienced." He rubbed the bottom of his chin, trying to remember the shop in the desperate blur of his search. "Some of the items in your window display were quite beautiful. But I must admit, by the horde of goods, I was worried you were part goblin."

"What?" Mara snapped, furrowing her brow. "A goblin? Are you serious?" She huffed. "Just when you start to act nice and normal, you go on and insult me."

"Mara."

"A *goblin* of all things?"

"I am not trying to insult you. I thought your shop had some nice things. I hardly knew you at the time."

"Poor Vareck, probably heartbroken that his mate was going to be such a vile creature. And you thought that was what I was? Goblins are filthy. And gross. It's like they never bathe. They're thieves, and they're hoarders, and they have such terrible personalities and tempers."

Corvo flicked his tail, shifting his head over on the pillow. "Wow, sounds just like you."

Mara scoffed, pushing the cushion off the nook. The cat scrambled to get away, laughing as she sat fuming.

Vareck rubbed at his temples, expelling a deep sigh. And here he thought they were making headway. What an improvement. "Mara, I did not—"

"I heard you the first time," she snapped. "It's fine."

The king crossed his arms, shaking his head. Of the few things he knew about a woman, he at least knew those words were opposite from the truth.

"I'm sorry, I didn't mean it that way."

"Sure."

Vareck sighed, letting his arms drop. He was about to speak further when a familiar growling and gurgling interrupted. Mara flushed, her hands moving down to hold her stomach, looking anywhere but at him.

"How about a truce? We could use some breakfast. I feed you, you forgive me."

"It's a start," Mara said hesitantly, turning towards him.

"Alright, what do you like to eat?" Vareck asked. He was about to suggest common meals within the castle walls when a hasty knock rapped against the door. The king turned, pulling on the handle to see who wanted to bother him now.

"Your Majesty," the guard quickly bowed at his presence, remaining in that state as he spoke. "Lady Elena is demanding a word with you. She sent me ahead to let you know she is on her way up." The guard stood, trying to catch his breath. Vareck stiffened, head shooting back towards Mara before looking back to the man in the hallway.

"No, that isn't necessary. I will meet with Lady Elena in the throne room. Tell her she does not need to stress herself of the travel." He turned his head towards Mara. "I'm sorry. I need to handle this. I will send for breakfast and try not to take long."

His eyes scanned the room for the cat. "Corvo, watch over Mara while I'm gone."

The cat huffed, letting out a big yawn before spreading his paws forward. "Babysitting? The girl can eat without being watched. She has the necklace on. It's not like she can go anywhere. Hey, why don't you send some food for me too?"

"Corvo."

"Alright, alright. Geez. Tell Elena I said hi. I know how much she adores me."

MARA

❄

After Vareck left, Mara went to the bed and busied herself fixing up the sheets. Making the bed, or futon, every morning had always been part of her routine. Getting back to some sense of normalcy now that she could move, speak, and walk around meant everything. She knew she needed to keep her wits about her if she was going to get through all of this.

Corvo happily hopped onto the covers, taking in the rewards of it being freshly made.

"Seriously, cat? I just straightened up."

"Beds are made for napping, Mara. Why else would you make it if not to use it?"

"Well, you're not wrong." She sighed, surrendering to Corvo's logic. She crawled on top of the blankets as well, leaning against the headboard as she watched him curl up on a pillow.

"What are you doing?"

"What's it look like I'm doing? I'm going to sleep on Vareck's pillow. He hates it when I do that. Makes it all the more satisfying. Especially when he sneezes."

Mara laughed, resting her hands on her stomach as its growling echoed the large room once more. As if hearing the call, two brownie servants entered pushing a cart with a large sterling silver dome. Mara grabbed for the spot on her leg where her dagger normally rested, even if it wasn't there.

What had surprised her was the servant's failure to knock. All the previous attendants thus far had done so. The only one who usually entered unannounced was the king. She nervously glanced between the two, eyes unsure until a delectable scent wafted to her nose.

"Hello, dearie! You poor starving thing. We have your brunch. Hope you're hungry," the first brownie spoke, a simple gray dress fitting her form. Black buttons ran down the sides as an apron sat tied around her waist. Mara wasn't sure what to say, eyes darting soon to the other man as he spoke up as well.

"King Vareck sent us to make you're taken care of." His outfit was similar in nature, having gray slacks and a matching vest. A white dress shirt sat underneath, and black buttons lined the front. As far as their appearance went, they were only slightly shorter than her and they almost looked like—

"We're twins. No need to be shy about it. I'm Gertrude, and this is my brother, Gin." The girl had brown pigtails that sat on the sides of her head, while her brother seemed more put together and stoic in nature. Gloves covered his hands and his brunette hair was cut short.

"Oh." She sat up, feeling a bit more at ease at their introductions. "My name is Mara."

"Mara, what a lovely name! Well, Mara. We have plenty of things on the cart. The king didn't know what you would like, so we just brought a little bit of everything." Gertrude laughed, pressing her hand to her chest as Gin removed the top dome of a silver platter. Both twins got to work immediately, Gin setting a tray in front of her and placing down plate after plate. Gertrude walked around the bed the long way, filling up a goblet of wine that she handed to Mara directly.

"This is . . . a lot. Thank you," Mara mumbled, trying to take in everything. Usually breakfast consisted of toast or even just coffee if she was running late to open the store. Before her sat eggs, potatoes, fresh bread and cheese, what appeared to be a sausage or other type of meat, some winter fruits, and even a few things she wasn't sure how to identify.

With the food laid out for her, the twins stood back on either side of the bed, giving her a small bow. "We hope you enjoy your meal," they said in unison.

"I—yeah, thanks." Mara replied, wrapping her fingers around the wine. The twins smiled back, resting with their hands in front of them. The odd thing was they kept standing there. Staring. Waiting. What did they want her to do? Were they waiting for her to eat? Did Vareck tell them to keep her company? It would be nice to talk to someone . . .

"Thank you. This is all very kind."

"Of course," Gertrude replied, continuously peppy in her tone.

Gin put a hand up to his chest. "If there is anything we can do to assist you, please let us know."

"This is perfect. Honestly." She set the wine down on the tray, eyes immediately trying to find something bacon-like. It was one of the best things about the human world and of course the fae wouldn't have it. She couldn't complain about the amazing spread, though. She grabbed a piece of the warm bread, spooning some egg and potato into it before folding it up and taking a big bite and letting out a pleasurable groan. "This is fantastic. This bread; the spice on these potatoes, oh my god, they're so good," she said around a mouthful of food.

"Oh good, I'm so glad you think so. There really is a lot you can do with a root vegetable, if you know what you're doing." Gertrude clasped her hands together, grinning from ear to ear.

"Do you cook for all of the castle?" Mara asked, taking another bite and holding her other hand beneath her makeshift sandwich.

"No, there's far too many to serve," Gin answered. "We focus on taking care of the needs solely of the king and the royal family."

Mara saw from her peripheral that Corvo was eyeing up the food, swishing his tail to the side.

"Did you want some?" Mara asked, side-eyeing the cat. He might be a cheeky bastard, but she had to live with him for the time being.

"Me? No. . . I think I feel another nap coming on. The cold here makes me so tired . . ." Corvo purred, trailing off as his eyes flitted closed.

"From the cold? You must be tired often," Mara mused.

"You have no idea." The cat closed his eyes, hiding his face between his front two legs.

She turned to the twin servants. "Would either of you like some breakfast? There's no way I can eat all of this myself."

"No, Lady Mara. Your kindness is appreciated, but this is all for you," Gertrude replied, her hair bouncing as she nodded her head. Mara took in the servant's words as she grabbed an apple slice from the corner.

"Is all of this grown here?" Mara asked, curious about the harvests with the raging war of cold outside.

"Most of it, yes. Sometimes we get some special treats from the human realm, like strawberries. We have greenhouses. Even then, the cold is too much. We mostly harvest what survives in the winter. Squashes, root vegetables, some winter fruits. It's the best we can do, but food becomes scarcer as the years pass by; the sun shining less and the cold becoming colder. Less crop surviving,"

Gin answered, the two seeming to switch back and forth when Mara asked them anything. But to not be able to use the land here to support their own people was concerning. What would Faerie do if it was ever cut off from the human realm? How could they continue to feed the people if even the greenhouses weren't enough?

Mara realized that this was her chance. While the twins were here, she could finally get some of the answers she so desperately wanted. "What is there to know about the king? Does he live up to the title and all of the rumors you hear?"

"We would have no job without King Vareck," Gin answered a second question in a row, breaking the chain of back and forth.

Mara frowned. Right. Should have known that there's still a bias. The tiniest of snores emitted from Corvo as he had already drifted off to sleep. Mara rolled her eyes. Finishing up with one more bite, she took a swig of the wine. Instead of the familiar warmth that alcohol brings, there was an odd cold that seeped into her veins. Even the wine brought a chill here.

Or maybe it was the cold that seeped into your skin over time. Corvo had just said that it made him tired. At the same time, she could feel her face heat up quickly, a new burning numbness crawling over her skin. She put down the glass, noticing that her vision began to blur at the edges. Was she dehydrated? Mara blinked, trying to shake it off, only it was getting worse.

Anxiety flared with a mix of slowing numbness.

HUNTED BY THE WINTER KING

Everything was too fast and too slow at the same time. "Did you poison me?" Mara slurred, trying to push herself up and off the bed. She barely made it half a foot before having to hold onto the covers. Kidnapped only to die by another's hand? This was perfect.

"Oh, don't be so dramatic," Gin chided, tilting his head to face her head on.

"Don't worry, we didn't poison you," Gertrude giggled.

"We just want to take you for a nice walk," Gin finished.

Mara slumped over, fighting to maintain consciousness. "Pair of fools you two are. If you wanted . . . wanted to kidnap me, there's . . . there's easier ways." She swallowed dryly, internally begging for the world around her to stop spinning. "Hell, I would have . . . gone . . . with you . . . at this . . ."

Laying on her side, she stared at the twins' faces as they watched her fall into oblivion, her words turned into incoherent mumbles as everything around her faded to black.

To be continued . . .

If you loved this book, please consider leaving a review on Amazon. This is Ariel's first novel and your reviews will help other readers decide whether they would like her books or not.

ABOUT THE AUTHOR

Ariel Hunter is an author of sexy fantasy.

She writes about alpha males, badass women, and the magical worlds they inhabit. She lives on the gulf coast with her husband, adorable—though potentially part demon—children, and furbabies of all sizes. When she's not writing, she is likely buried in a book, soaking in the sun, and eating tacos.
If you'd like to keep up with her new releases, please follow her on Amazon because she's antisocial and doesn't want to join social media. However, she is always happy to hear from adoring fans at authorarielhunter@gmail.com. She promises to try her very best to respond.

Printed in Great
Britain
by Amazon